STORIES OF JAPAN

Frances Little

ONE PEACE
BOOKS

Copyright © 2013 One Peace Books

The Lady of the Decoration was originally published in 1906 by The Century Co.; *The Lady and Sada San* was originally published in 1912 by The Century Co.

First edition published by One Peace Books, 2013
1 2 3 4 5 6 7 8 9 10

ISBN: 978-1-935548-34-8

Printed in the United States

Distribution by SCB Distributors
www.scbdistributors.com

For more information, contact:
One Peace Books
43-32 22nd Street, #204
Long Island City, NY 11101
www.onepeacebooks.com

Note: The content of this book adheres to the original text of both novels, so spelling, punctuation, etc., may differ from what is considered correct today.

Title Font: Sreda

CONTENTS

The Lady of the Decoration 5

The Lady and Sada San 135

THE LADY OF THE DECORATION

*To All
Good Sisters, and to Mine
in Particular*

SAN FRANCISCO, July 30, 1901.

My dearest Mate:

Behold a soldier on the eve of battle! I am writing this in a stuffy little hotel room and I don't dare stop whistling for a minute. You could cover my courage with a postage stamp. In the morning I sail for the Flowery Kingdom, and if the roses are waiting to strew my path it is more than they have done here for the past few years.

When the train pulled out from home and I saw that crowd of loving, tearful faces fading away, I believe that for a few moments I realized the actual bitterness of death! I was leaving everything that was dear to me on earth, and going out into the dark unknown, alone.

Of course it's for the best, the disagreeable always is. You are responsible, my beloved cousin, and the consequences be on your head. You thought my salvation lay in leaving Kentucky and seeking my fortune in strange lands. Your tender sensibilities shrank from having me exposed to the world as a young widow who is not sorry. So you "shipped me some-wheres East of Suez" and tied me up with a four years' contract.

But, honor bright, Mate, I don't believe in your heart you can blame me for not being sorry! I stuck it out to the last,—faced neglect, humiliations, and days and nights of anguish, almost losing my self-respect in my effort to fulfil my duty. But when death suddenly put an end to it all, God alone knows what a relief it was!

And how curiously it has all turned out! First my taking the Kindergarten course just to please you, and to keep my mind off things that ought not to have been. Then my sudden release from bondage, and the dreadful manner of it, my awkward position, my dependence,—and in the midst of it all this sudden offer to go to Japan and teach in a Mission school!

Isn't it ridiculous, Mate? Was there ever anything so absurd as my lot being cast with a band of missionaries? I, who have never missed a Kentucky Derby since I was old enough to know a bay from a sorrel! I guess old Sister Fate doesn't want me to be a one part star. For eighteen years I played pure comedy, then tragedy for seven, and now I am cast for a character part.

Nobody will ever know what it cost me to come! All of them were so terribly opposed to it, but it seems to me that I have spent my entire life going against the wishes of my family. Yet I would lay down my life for any one of them. How they have stood by me and loved me through all my blind blunders. I'd back my mistakes against anybody else's in the world!

Then Mate there was Jack. You know how it has always been with Jack. When I was a little girl, on up to the time I was married, after that he never even looked it, but just stood by me and helped me like a brick. If it hadn't been for you and for him I should have put an end to myself long ago. But now that I am free, Jack has begun right where he left off seven years ago. It is all worse than useless; I am everlastingly through with love and sentiment. Of course we all know that Jack is the salt of the earth, and it nearly kills me to give him pain, but he will get over it, they always do, and I would rather for him to convalesce without me than with me. I made him promise not to write me a line, and he just looked at me in that quiet, quizzical way and said: "All right, but you just remember that I'm waiting, until you are ready to begin life over again with me."

Why it would be a death blow to all his hopes if he married me! My widow's mite consists of a wrecked life, a few debts, and a worldly notion that a brilliant young doctor like himself has no right to throw away all his chances in order to establish a small hospital for incurable children. Whenever I think of his giving up that long-cherished dream of studying in Germany, and buying ground for the hospital instead, I just gnash my teeth.

Oh! I know that you think it is grand and noble and that I am horrid to feel as I do. Maybe I am. At any rate you will acknowledge that I have done the right thing for once in coming away. I seem to have been a general blot on the landscape, and with your help I have erased myself. In the meanwhile, I wish to Heaven my heart would ossify!

The sole power that keeps me going now is your belief in me. You have always claimed that I was worth something, in spite of the fact that I have persistently proven that I was not. Don't you shudder at the risk you are taking? Think of the responsibility of standing for me in a Board of Missions! I'll stay bottled up as tight as I know how, but suppose the cork *should* fly?

Poor Mate, the Lord was unkind when he gave me to you for a cousin.

Well it's done, and by the time you get this I will probably be well on my sea-sick way. I can't trust myself to send any messages to the family. I don't even dare send my love to you. I am a soldier lady, and I salute my officer.

On Ship-board. August 8th, 1901.

It's so windy that I can scarcely hold the paper down but I'll make the effort. The first night I came aboard, I had everything to myself. There were eighty cabin passengers and I was the only lady on deck. It was very rough but I stayed up as long as I could. The blue devils were swarming so thick around me that I didn't want to fight them in the close quarters of my state-room. But at last I had to go below, and the night that followed was a terror. Such a storm raged as I had never dreamed of, the ship rocked and groaned, and the water dashed against the port-holes; my bag played tag with my shoes, and my trunk ran around the room like a rat hunting for its hole. Overhead the shouts of the captain could be heard above the answering shouts of the sailors, and men and women hurried panic-stricken through the passage.

Through it all I lay in the upper berth and recalled all the unhappy nights of the past seven years; disappointment, heartache, disillusionment, disgust; they followed each other in silent review. Every tender memory and early sentiment that might have lingered in my heart was ruthlessly murdered by some stronger memory of pain. The storm without was nothing to the storm within, I felt indifferent as to the fate of the vessel. If she floated or if she sank, it was one and the same to me.

When morning came something had happened to me. I don't know what it was, but my past somehow seemed to belong to someone else. I had taken a last farewell of all the old burdens, and I was a new person in a new world.

I put on my prettiest cap and my long coat and went up on deck. Oh, my dear, if you could only have seen the sight that greeted me! It was the limpest, sickest crowd I ever encountered! They were pea-green with a dash of yellow, and a streak of black under their eyes, pale around the lips and weak in their knees. There was only one other woman besides myself who was not sick, and she was a missionary with short hair, and a big nose. She was going around with some tracts asking everybody if they were Christians. Just as I came up she tackled a big, dejected looking foreigner who was huddled in a corner.

"Brother, are you a Christian?"

"No, no," he muttered impatiently. "I'm a Norwegian."

Now what that man needed was a cocktail, but it was not for me to suggest it.

At table I am in a corner with three nice old gentlemen and one young German. They are great on story-telling, and I've told all of mine, most of yours and some I invented. One of the old gentlemen is a missionary; when he found that I was distantly connected with the fold he immediately called me "Dear Sister." If I were at home I should call him "Dear Pa," but I am on my good behavior.

The eating is fairly good, only sometimes it is so hot with curry and spice that it nearly takes my breath. My little Chinese waiter is entirely too solicitous for my comfort. No amount of argument will induce him to leave my plate until I have finished, after a few mouthfuls he whisks it away and brings me another relay. After pressing upon me dishes of every kind, he insists on my filling up all crevices with nuts and raisins, and after I have eaten, and eaten, he looks hurt, and says regretfully: "Missy sickee, no eatee."

There is one other person, who is just as solicitous. The little German watches my every mouthful with round solemn eyes, and insists upon serving everything to me. He looks bewildered when anyone tells a funny story, and sometimes asks for an explanation. He has been around the world twice, and is now going to China for three years for the Society of Scientific Research. He seems to think I am the greatest curio he has yet encountered in his travels.

The chief excitement of our trip so far has been the day in Honolulu. I wanted to sing for joy when we sighted

THE LADY OF THE DECORATION

land. The trees and grass never looked so beautiful as they did that morning in the brilliant sunshine. It took us hours to land on account of the red tape that had to be unwound, and then there was an extra delay of which I was the innocent cause. The quarantine doctor was inspecting the ship, and after I had watched him examine the emigrants, and had gotten my feelings wrought up over the poor miserable little children swarming below, I found a nice quiet nook on the shelter deck where I snuggled down and amused myself watching the native boys swim. The water on their bronze bodies made them shine in the sunlight, and they played about like a shoal of young porpoises. I must have stayed there an hour, for when I came down there was considerable stir on board. A passenger was missing and we were being held while a search of the ship was made. I was getting most excited when the purser, who is the sternest and best looking man you ever saw, came up and pounced upon me. "Have you been inspected?" he demanded, eyeing me from head to foot. "Not any more than at present," I answered meekly. "Come with me," he said.

I asked him if he was going to throw me overboard, but he was too full of importance to smile. He handed me over to the doctor saying: "Here is the young woman that caused the delay." Young woman, indeed! but I was to be crushed yet further for the doctor looked over his glasses and said: "Now how did we miss that?"

But on to Honolulu! I don't wonder people go wild over it. It is as if all the artists in all the world had spilled their colors over one spot, and Nature had sorted them out at her own sweet will. I kept wondering if I had died and gone to Heaven! Marvelous palms, and tropical plants, and all hanging in a softly dreaming silence that went to my head like wine.

I started out to see the city, with two old ladies and a girl from South Dakota, but Dear Pa and Little Germany joined the party. Oh! Mate how I longed for you! I wanted to tie all those frousy old freaks up in a hard knot and pitch them into the sea! The girl from South Dakota is a little better than the rest, but she wears a jersey!

There *are* real tailor-made people on board, but I don't dare associate with them. They play bridge most of the time and if I hesitated near them I'd be lost. I'll play my part, never fear, but I hereby swear that I will not dress it!

STILL ON BOARD. August 18th.

Dear Mate:

I am writing this in my berth with the curtains drawn. No I am not a bit sea-sick, just popular. One of the old ladies is teaching me to knit, the short-haired missionary reads aloud to me, the girl from South Dakota keeps my feet covered up, and Dear Pa and Little Germany assist me to eat.

The captain has had a big bathing tank rigged up for the ladies, and I take a cold plunge every morning. It makes

THE LADY OF THE DECORATION

me think of our old days at the cottage up at the Cape. Didn't we have a royal time that summer and weren't we young and foolish? It was the last good time I had for many a long day—but there, none of that!

Last night I had an adventure, at least it was next door to one. I was sitting up on deck when Dear Pa came by and asked me to walk with him. After several rounds we sat down on the pilot house steps. The moon was as big as a wagon wheel and the whole sea flooded with silver, while the flying fishes played hide and seek in the shadows. I forgot all about Dear Pa and was doing a lot of thinking on my own account when he leaned over and said:

"I hope you don't mind talking to me. I am very, very lonely." Now I thought I recognized a grave symptom, and when he began to tell me about his dear departed, I knew it was time to be going.

"You have passed through it," he said. "You can sympathize."

I crossed my fingers in the dark. "We are both seeking a life work in a foreign field—" he began again, but just here the purser passed. He almost stumbled over us in the dark and when he saw me and my elderly friend, he actually smiled!

Don't you dare tell Jack about this, I should never hear the last of it.

Can you realize that I am three whole weeks from home? I do, every second of it. Sometimes when I stop to think what I am doing my heart almost bursts! But then I am so used to the heartache that I might be lonesome without it; who knows?

If I can only do what is expected of me, if I can only pick up the pieces of this smashed-up life of mine and patch them into a decent whole that you will not be ashamed of, then I will be content.

The first foreign word I have learned is "Alohaoe," I think it means "my dearest love to you." Any how I send it laden with the tenderest meaning. God bless and keep you all, and bring me back to you a wiser and a gladder woman.

KOBE. August 18th, 1901.

Actually in Japan! I can scarcely believe it, even with all this strange life going on about me. This morning a launch came out to the steamer bringing Miss Lessing and Miss Dixon, the two missionaries in whose school I am to work. When I saw them, I must confess that my heart went down in my boots! Theirs must have done the same thing, for we stood looking at each other as awkwardly as if we belonged to different planets. The difference began with our heels and extended right on up to the crown of our hats. Even the language we spoke seemed different, and when I faced the prospect of living with such utter strangers, I wanted to jump overboard!

My fellow passengers suddenly became very dear, I clung to everything about that old steamer as the last link that

THE LADY OF THE DECORATION

bound me to America.

As we came down the gang plank, I was introduced to "Brother Mason" and "Brother White," and we all came ashore together. I felt for all the world like a convict sentenced to four years in the penitentiary. When we reached the Hotel, I fled to my room and flung myself on the bed. I knew I might as well have it out. I cried for two hours and thirty-five minutes, then I got up and washed my face and looked out of the window.

It was all so strange and picturesque that I got interested before I knew it. By and by Miss Lessing came in. Now that her hat was off I saw that she had a very sweet face with pretty dark hair and a funny little twinkle behind her eyes that made me think of you. She told me how she had come out to Japan when she was a young girl, and how she had built up the school, and all she longed to do for it. Then she said, "Your coming seems like the direct answer to prayer. It has been one of my dearest dreams to have a Kindergarten for the little ones, it just seems too good to be true!" And she looked at me out of her nice shining eyes with such gratitude and enthusiasm that I was ashamed of what I had felt.

After that Miss Dixon came up and they sat and watched me unpack my trunk. It took me about two minutes to find out that they were just like other women, fond of finery and pretty things and eager for news of the outside world. They examined all the dainty under clothes that sister had made for me, they marvelled over the high heeled slippers, and laughed at the big sleeves.

"Where are you going to wear all these lovely things?" asked Miss Dixon. And again my heart sank, for even my simple wardrobe, planned for the exigencies of school life, seemed strangely extravagant and out of place.

But I want to say right now, Mate, that if I stay here a thousand years I'll never come to jerseys and eight-year-old hats! I am going to subscribe to a good fashion paper, and at least keep within hailing distance of the styles.

It is too warm to go down to the school yet so we are to spend a week in the mountains before we start in for the fall term.

Dear Pa and Little Germany have been here twice in three hours but I saw them first.

Home letters will not arrive until next week, and I can scarcely wait for the time to come. I keep thinking that I am away on a visit and that I will be going back soon. I find myself saving things to show you, and even starting to buy things to bring home. I have a good deal to learn, haven't I?

Hieisan. August 28th, 1901

Fairy-land, real true fairy-land that we used to talk about up in the old cherry-tree at grandmother's! It's all so, Mate, only more bewitching than we ever dreamed.

I have been in little villages that dropped right out of

THE LADY OF THE DECORATION

a picture book. The streets are full of queer, small people who run about smiling, and bowing and saying pretty things to each other. It is a land where everybody seems to be happy, and where politeness is the first commandment.

Yesterday we came up the mountains in jinrickshas. The road was narrow, but smooth, and for over three hours the men trotted along, never halting or changing their gait until we stopped for lunch.

There is not much to a Japanese house but a roof and a lot of bamboo poles, but everything is beautifully clean. Before we had gotten down, several men and women came running out and bowing and calling "Ohayo, Ohayo" which means "good-morning." They ran for cushions and we were glad enough to sit on the low benches and stretch ourselves. Then they brought us delicious tea, and gathered around to see us drink it. It seems that light hair is a great curiosity over here, and mine proved so interesting that they motioned for me to take off my hat, and then they stood around chattering and laughing at a great rate. Miss Lessing said they wanted me to take my hair down, but would not ask it because of the beautiful arrangement. Shades of Blondes! I wish you could have seen it! But you *have* seen it after a hard set of tennis.

When we had rested an hour, and drunk tea, and bowed and smiled, we started out again, this time in a kind of Sedan chair, made of bamboo and carried on a long pole on the shoulders of two men. Now I have been up steep places but that trip beat anything I ever saw! I felt like a fly on a bald man's head! We climbed up, up, up, sometimes through woods that were so dense you could scarcely know it was day-time, and again through stretches of dazzling sunshine.

Just as I was beginning to wonder what had become of our luggage, we passed four women laughing and singing. Two of them had steamer trunks on their heads, and two carried huge kori. They did not seem to mind it in the least, and bowed and smiled us out of sight.

Another two hours' climb brought us to this village of camps called Hieisan. There are about forty Americans here, who are camping out for the summer, and I am the guest of a Dr. Waring and his wife from Alabama.

My tent is high above everything, on a great overhanging rock, and before me is a view that would be a fit setting for Paradise. This mountain is sacred to Buddha, and the whole of it is thick with temples and shrines, some of them nobody knows how old.

I have been trying to muster courage to get up at three o'clock in the morning to see the monkeys come out for breakfast. The mountains are full of them, but they are only to be seen at that hour.

There are some very pleasant people here, and I have made a number of friends. I am something of a conundrum, and curiosity is rife as to *why* I came. Mrs. Waring dresses me up and shows me off like a new doll, and the women consult me about making over their clothes.

I don't know why I am not perfectly miserable. The truth

is, Mate, I am having a good time! It's nice to be petted and treated like a child. It is good to be among plain, honest people, that live out doors, and have healthy bodies and minds.

I want to forget all that I learned about the world in the past seven years. I want to begin life again as a girl with a few illusions, even if they are borrowed ones. I know too much for my years and I'm determined to forget.

The home letters were heavenly. I've read them limber. I'll answer the rest to-morrow.

HIROSHIMA. Sept. 2nd, 1901.

At last after my wanderings I am settled for the winter. The school is a big structure, open and airy, and I have a nice room facing the east where you dear ones are. On two sides tower the mountains, and between them lies the magical Inland Sea. This is a great naval and military station, and while I write I can hear the bugle calls from the parade grounds.

I have a pretty little maid to wait on me and I wish you could see us talking to each other. She comes in, bows until her head touches the floor and hopes that my honorable ears and eyes and teeth are well. I tell her in plain English that I am feeling bully, then we both laugh. She is delighted with all my things, and touches them softly saying over and over: "It's mine to care for!"

There are between four and five hundred girls in the school and, until I get more familiar with the language, I am to work with the older girls who understand some English. You would smile to see their curiosity concerning me. They think my waist is very funny and they measure it with their hands and laugh aloud. One girl asked me in all seriousness why I had had pieces cut out of my sides, and another wanted to know if my hair used to be black. You see in all this big city I am the only person with golden tresses, and a green carnation would not excite more comment.

Yesterday we went shopping to get some curtains for my room. Such a crowd followed us that we could scarcely see what we were doing. When we went into the stores we sat on the floor and a little boy fanned us all the time we were making our selection.

Monday, Miss Lessing asked me to begin a physical culture class with the larger girls who are being trained for teachers, so I decided that the first lesson would be on *skipping*. It is an unknown art in Japan and the lack of it makes the Kindergarten work very awkward.

I took fourteen girls out on the porch and told them by signs and gestures to follow me. Then I picked up my skirts, and whistling a coon-song, started off. You never saw anything to equal their look of absolute astonishment! They even got down on their hands and knees to watch my feet. But they were game, and in spite of their tight kimonos and sandalled feet they made a brave effort to follow.

THE LADY OF THE DECORATION

The first attempt was disastrous, some fell on their faces, some went down on their knees, and all stumbled. I didn't dare laugh for the Japanese can stand anything better than ridicule. I helped and encouraged and cheered them on to victory. The next day there was a slight improvement, and by the third day they were experts. I found that they had spent the whole afternoon in practice! Now what do you suppose the result is? An epidemic of skipping has swept over Hiroshima like the measles! Men women and children are trying to learn, and when we go out to walk I almost have convulsions at the elderly couples we pass earnestly trying to catch the step!

I was so encouraged by this success that I taught the girls all sorts of steps and figures, even going so far as to teach them the *quadrille*! But my ambition led me a little too far. One day I came to class with a brand new step, which I had invented myself. It was rather giddy, but a splendid exercise. Well I headed the line and after the girls had followed me around the room twice I saw that they were convulsed with laughter! When I asked what was the matter, they explained between gasps that the step was the principal movement in the heathen dance given during festivals to the God of Beauty! My saints! Wouldn't some of my dear brethren do a turn if they knew!

Every afternoon I take about forty of the girls out for a walk. Our favorite stroll is along the moat that surrounds the old castle. It is almost always spilling over with lotus blossoms. The maidens, trotting demurely along in their rain-bow kimonos and little clicking sandals make a pretty picture. We have to pass the parade grounds of the barracks where twenty thousand soldiers are stationed, and I do wish you could see them trying to be modest, and yet peeping out of the corners of their little almond eyes in a way which is not peculiar to any particular country.

And the way they imitate me makes me afraid to breathe naturally. This thing of being a shining example is more than I bargained for. It is one of the few things in my checkered career that I have hitherto escaped.

Never mind, Mate, I couldn't be frivolous if I wanted to down here. Kobe would have proven fatal, for there are many foreigners there, and the temptation to have a good time would have been too much for me. I am rapidly developing into a hymn-singing sister, and the world and the flesh and the devil are shut up in the closet. Let us pray.

October 2nd, 1901.

At last, dear Mate, I am started at my own work with the babies and there aren't any words to tell you how cunning they are. There are eighty-five high class children in the pay kindergarten, and forty in the free. The latter are mostly of the very poor families, most of the mothers working in the fields or on the railroads. There are so many pitiful cases that one longs for a mint of money and a dozen hands to relieve them. One little girl of six comes every day with her blind baby brother strapped on her back. She is a tiny thing herself and yet that baby is never unstrapped from her back until night comes. When I first saw her old weazened face and her eagerness to play, I just took them both in my lap and cried!

One funny thing I must tell you about. From the first week that I got here, the children have had a nickname for me. I noticed them laughing and nudging each other on the street and in the school, and whenever I passed they raised their right hands in salute, and gave a funny little clucking sound. They seemed to pass the word from one to another until every youngster in the neighborhood followed the trick. My curiosity was aroused to such a pitch that I got an interpreter to investigate the matter. When he came to report, he smilingly touched my little enamelled watch, the one Jack gave me on my 16th birthday, and apologetically informed me that the children thought it was a decoration from the Emperor and they were saluting me in consequence! And they have named me "The Lady of the Decoration." Think of it, I have a title, and I am actually looked up to by these funny yellow babies as a superior being. They forget it some time though when we all get to playing together in the yard. We can't talk to each other, but we can laugh and romp together, and sometimes the fun runs high.

I am busy from morning until night. The two kindergartens, a big training class in physical culture, two Japanese lessons a day and prayers about every three minutes, don't leave many spare hours for homesickness. But the longing is there all the same, and when I see the big steamers out in the harbor and realize that they are coaling for *home*, I just want to steal aboard and stay there.

The language is something awful. I get my tongue in such knots that I have to use a corkscrew to pull it straight again. Just between you and me, I have decided to give it up and devote my time to teaching the girls to speak English instead. They are such responsive, eager little things, it will not be hard.

As for the country, I wouldn't dare to attempt a description. Sometimes I just *ache* with the beauty of it all! From my window I can see in one group banana, pomegranate, persimmon and fig trees all loaded with fruit. The roses are still in full bloom, and color, color everywhere. Across the river, the banks are lined with picturesque houses that look out from a mass of green, and above them are teahouses, and temples and shrines so old that even the moss is gray, and time has worn away the dates engraved upon the stones.

We spent yesterday at the sacred Island of Miyajima, which is about one hour's ride from here. The dream of it is still upon me and I wish I could share it with you. We went over in a sampan, a rude open boat rowed by two men in undress uniform. For half an hour we literally danced across the sea; everything was fresh and sparkling, and I was so glad to be alive and free, that I just sang for joy. Miss Leasing joined in and the boatmen kept time, smiling and nodding their approval.

The mountains were sky high, and at their base in a small crescent-shaped plain was the village with streets so clean and white you hated to walk on them. We stopped at the "House of the White Cloud" and three little maids took off our shoes and replaced them with pretty sandals. The whole house was of cedar and ebony and bamboo and it had been rubbed with oil until it shone like satin. On the floor was a stuffed matting with a heavy border of crimson silk, and in the corner of the room was a jar that came to my shoulder, full of wonderfully blended chrysanthemums. All the rooms opened upon a porch which hung directly above a roaring waterfall, and below us a dozen steps away stretched the sparkling sea, full of hundreds of sailing vessels and junks.

In the afternoon, we wandered over the island, visiting the old, old temples, listening to the mysterious wailing of the wind bells, feeding the deer and crane, and drinking in the beauty of it all. I felt like a disembodied spirit, traveling back, back over the centuries, into dim forgotten ages. The dead seemed close about me, yet they brought no gloom, for I too was dead. All afternoon I had the impression of trying to keep my consciousness from drifting into oblivion through the gate of this magical dream!

How you would enjoy it all, and read its deeper meaning, which is hidden from me. But even if I can't philosophize like a certain blessed old Mate of mine, I can *feel* until every nerve is a tingle with the thrill.

Good bye for a little while; I've stolen the time to write you this, and now it behooves me to hustle.

November 12th, 1901.

It's been a long while between "drinks," but I have been waiting until I could write a letter minus the groans. The truth is I have hit bottom good and hard and it is only today that I have come to the surface. When the exhilaration of seeing all the new and strange sights wore off, I began to sink in a sea of homesickness that threatened to put an end to the kindergarten business for good and all.

I worked like mad, and all the time I felt like one of these whizzing rockets that go rushing through the air and die out in a miserable little fizzle at the end. I can stand it in the daytime, but at night I almost go crazy. And you have no idea how many women do lose their minds out here. Nearly every year some poor insane creature has to be shipped home. You needn't worry about that though, if I had mind enough to lose I'd have lost it long ago. But to think of all my old ambitions and aspirations ending in the humble task of wiping Little Japan's nose!

I suppose you think I am pulling for the shore but I am not. I am steering my little craft right out in the billows It may be dashed to smithereens, and it may come safely home again, but in any case, I'll have the consolation of the Texas cowboy that "I've done my durndest!"

THE LADY OF THE DECORATION

By the way, what has become of Jack? He needn't have taken me so literally as never to send me a message even! You mentioned his having been at the Cape while you were there. Was he just as unsociable as ever? I can see him now lying flat on his back in the bottom of a boat reading poetry. I hate poetry, and when he used to quote his favorite passages I made parodies on them. Now *you* were always different. You'd rhapsodize with him to his heart's content.

Just here I had a lovely surprise. I looked out of the window and saw a coolie pull a little wagon into the yard and begin to unload. I couldn't imagine what was taking place but pretty soon Miss Dixon came in with both arms full of papers, pictures, magazines and letters. It was all my mail! I just danced up and down for joy. I guess you will never know the meaning of letters until you are nine thousand miles from home. And such dear loving encouraging letters as mine were! I am going to sit right down and read them all over again,

November 24th, 1901.

Clear sailing once more, Mate! In my last, I remember, I was blowing the fog horn pretty persistently.

The letters from home set me straight again. If ever a human being was blessed with a good family and good friends it is my unworthy self!

The past week has been unusually exciting. First we had

a wedding on hand. The bride is a girl who has been educated in the school, so of course we were all interested. Some time ago, the middle-man, who does all the arranging, came to her father and said a young teacher in the Government school desired his daughter in marriage. The father without consulting the girl investigated the suitor's standing, and finding it satisfactory, said yea. So little Otoya was told that she was going to be married, and the groom elect was invited to call.

I was on tiptoe with curiosity to see what would happen, but the meeting took place behind closed doors. Otoya told me afterwards that she had never seen the young man until he entered the room, but they both bowed three times, then she served tea while her mother and father talked to him. "Didn't you talk to him at all?" I asked. She looked horrified. "No, that would have been most immodest!" she said. "But you peeped at him," I insisted. She shook her head, "That would have been disgrace." Now that was three months ago and she hadn't seen him until Monday when they were married.

At our suggestion they decided to have an American wedding and I was appointed mistress of ceremonies. It was great fun, for we had a best man, besides brides-maids and flower girls, and Miss Lessing played the Wedding March for them to enter. The arrangements were somewhat difficult owing to the fact that the Japanese consider it the height of vulgarity to discuss anything pertaining to the bride or the wedding. They excused me on the ground that I was a foreigner.

The affair was really beautiful! The little bride's outer garment was the finest black crepe, but under it, layer after layer, were slips of rainbow tinted cob-web silk that rippled into sight with every movement she made. And every inch of her trousseau was made from the cocoons of worms raised in her own house, and was spun into silk by her waiting maids.

After the excitement of the wedding had subsided, we had a visitation from forty Chinese peers. They came in a cavalcade of kuramas, gorgeously arrayed, and presenting an imposing appearance. I ran for the poker for I thought maybe they had come to finish "Us Missionaries." But, bless you, they had heard of our school and our kindergarten and had come for the Chinese Government to investigate ways and means. They made a tour of the school, ending up in the kindergarten. The children were completely overpowered by these black-browed, fierce-looking gentlemen, but I put them through their paces. The visitors were so pleased that they stayed all morning and signified their unqualified approval. When they started to leave, I asked the interpreter if their gracious highnesses would permit my unworthy self to take their honorable pictures.

Would you believe it? Those old fellows puffed up like pouter pigeons, and giggled and primped like a lot of school girls! They stood in a row and beamed upon me while I snapped the kodak. If the picture is good, I'll send you one.

This morning I had to teach Sunday School. I'll be praying in public next. I see it coming. The lesson was "The Prodigal Son," a subject on which I ought to be qualified to speak. The Japanese youths understood about one word out of three, but they were giving me close attention. I was expounding with all the earnestness in me when suddenly I remembered a picture Jack used to have. It was of a lean little calf tearing down the road, while in the distance was coming a lazy looking tramp. Underneath was the legend:

> "Run, bossy, run,
>   Here comes the Prodigal Son."

That settled my sermon, so I told the boys a bear story instead.

How I should love to drop in on you to-night and sit on the floor before the fire and pow-wow! I'll be an awful back number when I come home, but just think how entertaining I'll be! I have enough good dinner stories to last through the rest of my life!

For heaven's sake send me some hat pins, nice long ones with pretty heads. And if you are in New York this winter please get me two bottles of that violet extract that I always use.

My dearest love to all, and a hundred kisses to the blessed children at home. Don't you *dare* let them forget me.

THE LADY OF THE DECORATION

November 27th, 1901.

I told you it would come! My prophetic soul foresaw it. I had to lead the prayer in chapel this morning. And I play the organ in Sunday School and listen to two Japanese sermons on Sunday.

I tell you, Mate, this part of the work goes sadly against the grain. They say you get used to hanging if you just hang long enough, so I suppose I'll become reconciled in time.

You ask me *why* I do these things. Well you see it's all just like a big work shop, where everybody is working hard and cheerfully and yet there is so much work waiting to be done, that you don't stop to ask whether you like it or not.

I can't begin to tell you of the hopelessness of some of the lives out here. Just think of it! Women working in the stone quarries, and in the sand pits and on the railroads, and always with babies tied on their backs, and the poor little tots crippled and deformed from the cramped position and often blind from the glare of the sun.

What I am crazy to do now is to open another free kindergarten in one of the poorest parts of the city. It would cost only fifty dollars to run it a whole year, and I mean to do it if I have to sell one of my rings. It is just glorious to feel that you are actually helping somebody, even if that somebody is a small and dirty tribe of Japanese children. I get so discouraged and blue sometimes that I don't know what to do, but when a little tot comes up and slips a very soiled hand into mine and pats it and lays it against his cheek and hugs it up to his breast and says, "Sensei, Sensei," I just long to take the whole lot of them to my heart and love them into an education!

They don't know the word love but they know its meaning, and if I happen to stop to pat a little head, a dozen arms are around me in a minute, and I am almost suffocated with affection. One little fellow always calls me "Nice boy" because that is what I called him.

We are having glorious weather, cold in doors but warm outside. The chrysanthemums and roses are still blooming, and the trees are heavily laden with fruit. The persimmons grow bigger than a coffee cup and the oranges are tiny things, but both are delicious. Chestnuts are twice as big as ours, and they cook them as a vegetable.

You'll be having Thanksgiving soon, and you will all go up to Grandmother's, and have a jolly time together. Have them fix a plate for me, Mate, and turn down an empty glass. Nobody will miss me as much as I will miss my poor little self.

What jolly Thanksgivings we have had together! The gathering of the clans, the big dinner, and the play at night. Not exactly a play, was it, Mate? More of a vaudeville performance with you as the stage manager, and I as the soubrette. Do you remember the last reunion before I was married? I mean the time I was Lady Macbeth and gave a skirt dance, and you did lovely stunts from Grand

THE LADY OF THE DECORATION

Opera. Have you forgotten Jack's famous parody on "My Country 'Tis of Thee?"

> "My turkey, 'tis of thee,
> Sweet bird of cranberry,
> Of thee I sing!
> I love thy neck and wings,
> Legs, back and other things," etc, etc.

There goes the bell, and here go I. I can appreciate the feelings of a fire engine!

Christmas Day, 1901.

Had somebody told you last Christmas, as we trimmed the big tree and made ready for the family gathering, that this Christmas would find me in a foreign country teaching a band of little heathens, wouldn't you have thought somebody had wheels in his head?

And yet it is true, and I have only to lift my eyes to realize fully that I am really in the flowery kingdom. The plum blossoms are in full bloom and the roses too, while a thick frost makes everything sparkling white in the sunshine. The mountains have put on a thin blue veil trimmed in silver, and over all is a turquoise sky.

And best of all, everybody—I speak figuratively—is happy. It may be that some poor little waif is hungry, having had only rice water for breakfast, it may be some sad hearts are beating under the gay kimonos, and it *may* be, Mate dear, that somebody, a stranger in a strange land, can't keep the tears back, and is longing with all her mind and soul and body for home and her loved ones. But never you mind, nobody knows it but you and me and a bamboo tree!

This afternoon we are going to have tea for the Mammas and Papas, and I am going to put on my prettiest clothes and do my yellow locks in their most fetching style.

I shall lock up tight, way down deep, all heartaches and longings and put on my best smile for these dear little people who have given to me, a stranger, such full measure of their sympathy and friendship, who, in the big service last month, when giving thanks for all the great blessings of the past year, named the new Kindergarten teacher first.

Do you wonder that I am happy and miserable and homesick and contented all at the same time?

The box I sent home for Christmas was a paltry offering compared to what I wanted to send, but the things were bought with the first money I ever earned. They are packed in so tight with love that I doubt if you ever get them out.

Our Christmas dinner was not exactly a success. We invited all the foreigners in Hiroshima, twelve in number, and everybody talked a great deal and laughed at everybody's stale jokes, and pretended to be terribly hilarious. But there was a pathetic droop to every mouth, and not a soul referred to *home*. Each one seemed to realize that the mere mention of the word would break up the party.

THE LADY OF THE DECORATION

I tell you I am beginning to look with positive reverence on the heroism of some of these people! Tears and regrets have no place here; desire, ambition, love itself is laid aside, and only taken out for inspection perhaps in the dead hours of the night. If heart breaks come, as come they must, there is no crying out, no rebellion, just a stiffer lip and a firmer grip and the work goes on.

I wish I was like that, but I'm not. If Nature had put more time on my head and less on my heart, she would have turned out a better job.

I put a pipe in the box for Jack. If you think I ought not to have done it, don't give it to him. As old Charity used to say, "I don't want to discomboberate nobody." Only I hope he won't think I am ungrateful and indifferent.

NAGASAKI. January 14th, 1902.

Now aren't you surprised at hearing from me in Nagasaki? I am certainly surprised at being here! One of the teachers at the school, Miss Dixon, Was taken sick and had to come here to see a doctor. I was lucky enough to be asked to come with her.

I am so excited over being in touch with civilization again that I can't sleep at night! The transports and all the steamers stop here, and every type of humanity seems to be represented. This morning when I went out to mail a letter, there were two Sikhs in uniform in front of me, at my side was a Russian, behind me two Chinamen and a Japanese, while a Frenchman stepped aside for me to pass, and an Irishman tried to sell me some vegetables!

Miss Dixon had to go to the Hospital for a few days, though her trouble is nothing serious, and I accepted an invitation from Mrs. Ferris, the wife of the American Consul, to spend a few days with her.

And oh! Mate, if you only *knew* the time I have had! If I weren't a sort of missionary-in-law I would quote Jack and say it has been "perfectly damn gorgeously." If you want to really enjoy the flesh-pots just live away from them for six months and then try them!

The night I came, the Ferrises gave me a beautiful dinner, and I wore evening dress for the first time in two years, and was as thrilled as a debutante at her first ball! It was so good to see cut glass and silver, and to hear dear silly worldly chatter that I grew terribly frivolous. Plates were laid for twenty, and who do you suppose was on my right? The severe young purser who was on the steamer I came over in! His ship is coaling in the harbour and he is staying with the Ferrises, who are old friends of his. He is so solemn that he almost kills me. If he weren't so good looking I could let him alone, but as it is I can't help worrying the life out of him.

The dinner was most elaborate. After the oysters, came a fish nearly three feet long all done up in sea-weed, then a big silver bowl was brought in covered with pie-crust. When the carver broke the crust there was a flutter of

THE LADY OF THE DECORATION

wings, and "four and twenty black birds" flew out. This it seems was done by the Japanese cook as a sample of his skill. All sorts of queer courses followed, served in the most unique manner possible.

After dinner they begged me to sing, and though I protested violently, they got me down at the piano. I didn't get up any more until the party was over for they made me sing every song I knew and some I didn't. I sang some things so hoary with age that they were decrepit! The purser so far forgot himself as to ask me to sing "My Bonnie lies over the Ocean"! I did so with great expression while he looked pensively into the fire. Since then I have called him, "My Bonnie," and he *hates* me.

The next day we went out to services on board the battleship "Victor." The ship had been on a long cruise and we were the first American women the officers had seen for many a long day. They gave us a rousing welcome you may be sure. Through some mistake they thought I was a "Miss" instead of a "Mrs." and I shamelessly let it pass. During service I heard little that was said for the band was playing outside and flags were flying and I was feeling frivolous to the tip of my toe! I guess I am still pretty young, for brass buttons are just as alluring as of old.

When the Admiral heard I was from Kentucky, he invited us to take tiffin with him, and we exchanged darkey stories and the old gentleman nearly burst his buttons laughing. After tea, he showed us over the ship, making the sailors line up on deck for our benefit. "Tell the band to play 'Old Kentucky Home,'" he ordered.

"You'll lose a passenger if you do!" I cried, "for one note of that would send me overboard!"

He was so attentive that I had little chance to talk to the young officers I met. But several of them have called since, and I have been out to a lot of teas and dinners and things with them.

The one I like best is a young fellow from Vermont. He is very clever and jolly and we have great fun together. In fact, we are such chums that he showed me a picture of his fiancée. He is very much in love with her, but if I were in her place I would try to keep him within eye-shot.

We will probably go home to-morrow as Miss Dixon is so much better. I am glad she is better, but I could have been reconciled to her being mildly indisposed for a few days longer.

I forgot to thank you for the kodak book you sent Christmas; between the joy of seeing all the familiar faces, and the bitterness of the separation, and the absurdity of your jingles, I nearly had hysterics! I almost felt as if I had had a visit home! The old house, the cabin, the cherry tree, and all the family even down to old black Charity, the very sight of whom made me hungry for buckwheat cakes, all, all gave me such joy and pain that it was hard to tell which was uppermost.

It's worth everything to be loved as you all love me, and I am willing to go through anything to be worthy of it. I have had more than my share of hard bumps in life, but,

THE LADY OF THE DECORATION

thank Heaven, there was always somebody waiting to kiss the place to make it well. There isn't a day that I haven't some evidence of this love; a letter, a paper, a book that reminds me that I'm not forgotten.

A note has just come from his Solemn Highness, the purser, asking me to go walking with him! I am going to try to be nice to him but I know I won't! He is so young and so serious that I can't resist shocking him. He doesn't approve of giddy young widows that don't look sorry! Neither do I. In two days I return to the fold. Until then "My Bonnie" beware!

Hiroshima, February 19th, 1902.

After a sleepless night I got up this morning with a splitting headache. I have been back in the traces for a month, and I am beginning to feel like a poor old horse in a tread mill, not that I don't love the work, but oh! Mate, I am so lonesome, lonesome, lonesome. I think I used up so much sand when I first came that the supply is running low.

> "All day there is the watchful world to face
> The sound of tears and laughter fill the air.
> For memory there is but scanty space
> Nor time for any transport of despair.
> But, Love, the pulse beats slow, the lips turn white
> Sometimes at night!"

Perhaps when I am old and gray and wrinkled I'll be at peace. But think of the years in between! I have been cheated of the best that life holds for a woman, the love of a good husband, the love of her children, and the joys of a home.

The old world shakes its finger and says "you did it yourself." But, Mate, I was only eighteen, and I didn't know the real from the false. I staked my all for the prize of love, and I lost. Heaven knows I've paid the penalty, but I'd do it over again if I thought I was right. The difference is that then I was a child and knew too little, and now I am a woman and know too much.

Sometimes the hymn-singing and praying, and "Sistering" and "Brothering" get on my nerves, until I almost scream, but when I remember how heavenly good to me they are I'm all contrition. I have even been invited to write for the Mission papers, now isn't that sufficient glory for any sinner?

Your letters are such comforts to me! I read them over and over and actually know parts of them by heart! Since I was a little girl I have had a burning desire to win your approval. I remember once when you said I was stronger than the little boy next door I sprained my back trying to prove, it. And now when you write those lovely things about me and tell me how good and brave I am, why I'd sprain something worse than my back to be worthy of your approval!

But my courage doesn't always ring true, Mate, sometimes it's a brass ring. If you want to hear of true heroism, just listen to this story. There was a little American Missionary, who was going home to stay after twenty years of hard service. At the request of the board she stopped off at the Leper Colony in order to make a report. Soon after she reached home, she discovered a small white spot on her hand, and on consulting a physician, found it was leprosy. Without breathing a word of it to anyone, she bade her family and friends a cheerful good-bye, and came straight back to that Leper Colony, where she took up her work among the outcasts. Never an outcry, never a groan, not even a plea for sympathy! Now how is that for a soldier lady?

It is quite cold to-day and I am indulging in the luxury of a roaring fire. You know the natives use little stoves that they carry around with them, and call "hibachi." But cold as it is, the yard is full of roses and the tea-plants are gorgeous. I don't wonder that the climate gets mixed, out here. Everything else is hind part before.

What do you suppose I've been longing for all day? A good saddle horse? I feel that a brisk canter would set me straight in a short time. But the only horse in Hiroshima is a mule. A knock-kneed, cross-eyed old mule that bitterly resents the insult of being hitched to something that is a cross between a wheelbarrow and a baby buggy. The driver stands up for the excellent reason that he has no place to sit down! We tried this coupé once for the fun and experience. We got the experience all right but I am not so sure about the fun. We jolted along through the narrow streets scraping first against one house, then against another, while our footman, oh yes we had a footman, ran beside the thoroughbred to help him up when he stumbled.

To-morrow we are to have company. A Salvation Army lassie comes down from Tokio with a brass band. It is the second time in the history of the town that the people have had a chance to hear a brass band, and they are greatly thrilled. I must say I am a bit excited myself; Miss Lessing says she is going to keep me in sight, for fear I will follow the drum away. She needn't worry. I am through following anything in this world but my own nose.

Hiroshima, March 25, 1902.

I am absolutely walking on air today! Just when I thought my cherished dream of a free kindergarten would have to be given up, the checks from home came! You were a trump to get them all interested, and it was beautiful the way they responded. Only *why* did you tell Jack? He oughtn't to have sent so much. I'd send it back if I weren't afraid of hurting him.

My head is simply spinning with plans! We are going to open the school right away and there are hundreds of things to be done. In spite of my home-sickness, and loneliness and longing for you loved ones, I wouldn't come home now if I could! It is the feeling that I am needed here, that a big work will go undone, if I don't do it, that simply puts my little wants and desires right out of the question!

Yesterday we had a mothers' meeting, and I have not stopped laughing over it yet! It seems that the mothers considered it proper to show their appreciation by absolute solemnity. After tea and cake were served they sat in funeral silence. Not a word nor a smile could we get out of them. When I couldn't stand it another minute, I told Miss Lessing I was going to break the ice if I went under in the effort. By means of an interpreter, I told the mothers that we were going to try an American amusement and would they lend their honorable assistance? Then I called in thirty of the school girls and told each one to ask a mother to skip. They were too polite to decline, so to the tune of "Mr. Johnson, Turn Me Loose," the procession started. Miss Dixon couldn't stay in the room for laughing. The old and the young, and the fat and the thin caught the spirit of it and went hopping and jumping around the circle in great glee. After that, old ladies and all played "Pussy Wants a Corner," and "Drop the Handkerchief," and they laughed and chattered like a lot of children. They stayed four hours, and we are still picking up hair ornaments!

Up over my table I have the little picture you sent of the "Lane that turned at last." You always said my lane would turn, and it *has* turned into a broad road bordered by cherry-blossoms and wistaria. But, Mate, you needn't think there are no more mudholes, for there are. When I see them ahead, I climb the fence and walk around!

I am getting quite thrilled these days over the prospect of war. The soldiers are drilling by the hundreds, and the bugles are blowing all day. It makes little thrills run up and down my back, but Miss Lessing says nothing will come of it, that Japan is always getting ready for a scrap. But the Trans-Siberian Railway has refused all freight because it is too busy bringing soldiers and supplies to Vladivostock.

Now speaking of Vladivostock reminds me of a plan that has been suggested for next summer. Miss Dixon, the teacher who was sick, is going to Russia and is crazy for me to go with her. It wouldn't be much more expensive than staying in Japan, and would be tremendously interesting. Don't mention it to anybody at home, but write me if you approve.

I wish you could have peeped into my room last night. Four or five of the girls slipped in after the silence bell had rung, and we sat around the fire on the floor and drank tea while I showed them my photographs. They made such a pretty picture, with their gay gowns and red cheeks, and they were so thrilled over all my things. The pictures from home interested them most of all, especially the one of you and Jack which I have framed together. At first they thought you must be married, and when I said no, they decided that you were lovers, so I let it go.

After they went to bed, I sat and looked at the two pictures in the double frame and wondered how it was after all that you and Jack *hadn't* fallen in love with each other! You both live with your heads in the clouds; I should think you would have bumped into each other long before this. He told me once that you had fewer faults than any woman he had ever known. Telling me of other people's virtues was one of Jack's long suits.

My last minute of grace is gone, so I must say goodnight. I am getting up at five o'clock these mornings in order to get in all that I want to do.

HIROSHIMA, May 31, 1902.

Under promise that I will not write a long letter, I am allowed to begin one to you this morning. Miss Lessing wrote you last week that I had been sick. The truth is I tried to do too much, and paid up for it by staying in bed two whole weeks. Perhaps I will acquire a little sense in the next world; I certainly haven't in this! Japan wasn't made for restless, energetic people. If you can't learn to be lazy, you can't last long.

I can never tell you how good Miss Lessing has been, sleeping right by me, taking care of me and loving me like I was her own child. The girls too, have been so good sending me gifts almost every hour in the day. One little girl got up at prayers the other night, and, folding her hands, said: "Oh Lord, please make the Skipping Sensei well, and help me to keep my mouth shut so it will be quiet, for she has been good to us and we all do love her much." Heaven knows the "Skipping Sensei" needs all the prayers of the congregation!

Just as soon as school is over, Miss Dixon and I start for Russia. It's a good thing that vacation is near for I am tired of being a Missionary lady, and a school-marm, in fact I am tired of being good.

Don't worry about me, for I am all right. I've just run down and need a little fun to wind me up for another year.

Kobe, July 16, 1902.

Does July 16th mean anything to you? It does to me. Just one year ago today the gates of that old Union Depot shut between me and all that was dear to me, and I went out into the big world to fight my big fight alone. Well, I am still fighting, Mate, and probably will be to the end of the campaign.

As you see I am in Kobe waiting for my pass-port to go to Russia. If there is anything you want to know about pass-ports just apply to me. With all confidence, I sailed down to the Consulate and was met by a pair of legs attached to a huge mustache and the funniest little button of a head you ever saw. I think the Lord must have laughed when he got through making that man! He was horribly bored with life in general, and me in particular. He motioned me wearily to a chair beside a table, and, handing me a paper, managed to sigh: "Fill in."

The questions were about like this: Who was your father?

THE LADY OF THE DECORATION

What are you doing out of your own country? Was anybody in your family ever hung? How many teeth have you?

I wrote rapidly until I got to "When were you born?" Button-Head was standing by me, so I looked up at him helplessly and told him that was one thing I *never* could remember. He said I would have to, and I said I couldn't. He pranced around for fifteen minutes, and I pretended to be racking my brain.

Then he handed me a Bible, and said in a stern voice: "Swear." I told him that I couldn't, that I never had sworn, that ladies didn't do it in America, wouldn't he please do it for me?

About this time Miss Dixon spoiled the fun by laughing, so I had to behave. After we had spent two hours and three dollars in that dingy old office, we departed, but our troubles were not over. No sooner had we reached the hotel than Button-Head appeared with more papers. "You failed to describe yourself," he mournfully announced, handing me another slip.

I had not had my dinner and I was cross, but I seized a pen determined to make short work of it. How tall? Easily told. Black or white? Very easy. Kind of chin? Round and rosy. Shape of face? Depends on time and place. Hair? Pure gold. Eyes? Now I knew they were green but that did not sound poetic enough so I appealed to Dixie. She thought for a while, then said, "Not gray nor brown, I have it, they are syrup colored!" So I put it down along with a lot of other nonsense.

Now the papers have to be sent to Tokyo for approval, then back here again where I will have to do some more signing and swearing. Isn't this enough to discourage people from ever going anywhere?

The news about the sailboat is great. How many of you will be up at the Cape this summer? Is Jack going? When I think of the starlight nights out in the boat, and the long lazy mornings on the beach, I get absolutely faint with longing. Heretofore I haven't *dared* to enjoy things, and now, when I might, I am an exile heading for Siberia! Oh, well! perhaps there will be starlight nights in Siberia, who knows?

VLADIVOSTOCK, SIBERIA, August 16, 1902.

If I should write all I wanted to say this morning, my letter would reach across the Pacific! I didn't believe it was possible for me ever to have such a good time again.

When we came, we brought a letter of introduction to a Mrs. Heath. She has a beautiful big house, and a beautiful big heart, and she took us right into both.

The day after we arrived, I was standing on her piazza looking down the bay, when I saw a battle-ship come sailing in under a salute of seventeen guns from the fort. It turned out to be the "Victor," and you never knew such rejoicing. Mrs. Heath knows all the navy people and her house is a favorite rendezvous. Before night, we had met

THE LADY OF THE DECORATION

many old acquaintances, among them my Nagasaki friend, "Vermont."

It has been tremendously jolly and I can't deny that I have been outrageously frivolous for a missionary! But to save my life I can't conjure up the ghost of a regret! And what is more, I have been contaminating Dixie! I have kept her in such a giddy whirl that she says I have paralysed her conscience! I have dressed her up and trotted her along to lunches, teas and dinners, to concerts on sea and land, and once, Oh! awful confession, I bulldozed her into going to the theatre! The consequence is that she has gotten entirely well and looks ten years younger. Her chief trouble was that she had surrounded herself with a regular picket fence of creed and dogma, and was afraid to lift her eyes for fear she would catch a glimpse through the cracks, of the beautiful world which God meant for us to enjoy. It gave me particular joy to pull a few palings off that picket fence!

Most of my time is spent on the water with Vermont. I don't find it half bad out on the bewitching Uzzuri Bay when the moon is shining and the music floats over the water, to discuss love with a fascinating youth!

What does it matter if he is talking about "the other one"? Don't you suppose that I am glad to know that somewhere in this wide world there's a man that can be loyal to his sweetheart even though she is ten thousand miles away?

I ask occasional questions and don't listen to the answers, and he pours out his confessions and thinks I am lovely.

He really is one of the dearest fellows I ever met, and I am glad for that other girl with all my heart.

I like several of the other men very much but they bother me with questions. They refuse to believe that I am connected with a mission, and consider it all as a huge joke.

I wish you could see this place. It is built in terraces up the greenest of mountains and forms a crescent around the bay. Everybody seems to be in uniform of some kind, and soldiers and sailors are at every turn. The streets are a glittering panorama of strange color and form. At night everything is ablaze, bands playing, uniforms glittering, and flags flying. It is all just one intense thrill of life and rhythm, and the cloven foot of my worldliness never fails to keep time.

But when daylight comes and all the sordid ugliness is revealed, disgust takes the place of fascination. The streets are crowded with thousands of degraded Chinese and Koreans, who, even in their brutality, are not as bad as the ordinary Russians.

Through this mass of poverty and degradation dash handsome carriages filled with richly clad people. The drivers wear long blue plush blouses with red sleeves and belt, and trousers tucked in high boots. On their heads they wear funny little hats that look as if they had been sat on. They generally stand up while driving and lash the poor horses into a dead run from start to finish. Many of them are ex-convicts and can never leave Siberia. If their cruelty to horses is any criterion of their cruelty to their fellow men, I can't help thinking they deserve their punishment.

I won't dare to mail this letter until I get out of Russia for they are so cranky about their blessed old country. They would not even let me have a little flag to send to the boys at home! I found out to-day that a policeman comes every day to see what we have been doing, what hours we keep, etc. In fact every movement is watched, and one day when we returned to the hotel, we found that all our possessions had been searched, and the police had even left their old cigar stumps among our things! The more you see of Russia, the more deeply you fall in love with Uncle Sam!

Several days ago Mrs. Heath gave us a tennis-tea and we had a jolly time. The tea was served under the trees from a steaming samovar, around which gathered representatives of many nations. There were many unpronounceable gentlemen, and one real English Lord, who considered Americans, "frightfully amusing."

I thought I had forgotten how to play tennis but I hadn't. That undercut that Jack taught us won me a reputation.

It is only when I stop to think, that I realize how far I am from home! When I wonder where you all are this minute, and what you are doing, I feel as if I were on a visit to the planet Mars, and had no communication whatever with the world.

Think of me, Mate, in Siberia, eating fish with a spoon, and drinking coffee from a glass! Verily, when old Sister Fate found she could not down me, she must have decided to play pranks with me!

My box of new clothes arrived just before I started, and I have had use for everything. When I get on the white coat suit and the white hat, I feel like a dream.

The weather is simply glorious, like our best October days at home. Nothing could be more unlike than Russia and Japan! one is a great oil painting, tragic, majestic, grand, while the other is an exquisitely dainty water color full of sunshine and flowers.

Callers have come so I must close. Life is a very pretty game after all, especially when you get wise enough to look on.

VLADIVOSTOCK, SIBERIA, September 1, 1902.

Just a short letter to tell you that we leave Vladivostock to-night. I am all broken up; it has been the happiest summer that I have had for years and I can't bear to think of it being over.

It has been so long since Peace and I have been acquainted that I hardly yet dare look her full in the face for fear she will take flight and leave me in utter darkness again. Even if she has not come to live with me, she is at least my next door neighbor, and I offer her incense that she may abide.

Now I might as well confess that if it were not for Memory there is no telling what Peace might do! Poor old

THE LADY OF THE DECORATION

Memory! I'd like to throttle her sometime and bury her in a deep hole. Yet she has served me many a good turn, and often laid a restraining hand on impulse and thought. But she is like a poor relation, always turning up at the wrong time!

For instance, on a gorgeous moonlight night on the Uzzuri Bay when you are out in a sampan with a pigtail who neither sees nor hears, and your companion is clever enough to be fascinating and daring enough to say things he "hadn't oughter," and the music and the moonlight gets into your head, and you feel young and reckless and sentimental, then all of a sudden Memory recalls another moonlight night when the youth and the romance weren't merely make believe, and your mind travels wearily over the intervening years, and you sit up straight and look severe and put your hands behind you!

Oh! I am clinging to my ideal, Mate, never fear. I've held on to her garments until they are tattered and torn. You introduced me to her and I have never lost sight of her entirely.

This afternoon the Victor sailed for the Philippines. As she passed Mrs. Heath's cottage where we had all promised to be, she dipped her colors. I felt pretty blue for I knew my good times were on board, and were sailing out of sight.

I am now at the hotel, trunk and boxes packed, waiting to start. Cinderella is not going to wait for the stroke of twelve; she has donned her sober garments and is ready to be whisked back to the cinders on the hearth. I am glad hard work is ahead; a solid grind seems necessary for my soul's salvation.

Farewell, vain earth! I love you not wisely but too well.

Why can't people be nice to one without being too nice? And why can't you be horrid to people without being too horrid? Selah.

HIROSHIMA, October 10, 1902.

Dear Old Mate:

I am so dead tired to-night that I could not tell what part of me ached the most! But the spirit moves me to unburden my soul and I feel that I must write you. For this is one of my *dream* nights, and I have so many in Japan, when my old shell is too exhausted to move, and so permits my soul to wander where it will, a dream night, when the moon is its silveriest and biggest and I want to hug it for I know that twelve hours before it looked down on my loved ones, and now it comes to make more beautiful this fairy land, hiding the scars and ugly places, touching the pine trees with silver points, and glorifying the old Temples, till one wonders if they *could* have been made by hands. A night when the white robed priests are doing honor to some "heathen idol" and must needs call his wandering attention by the stroke of the deep toned bell, which sends its music far across sleeping Japan, out into the wonderful sea.

I don't know what comes over me such nights as these. I don't seem to be me at all! I can lie most of the night, wide awake, yet unconscious of my surroundings, and dream dreams. I live through all the joyful days of childhood, then through the sorrowful days of womanhood when I was learning how to live, through the years of heartache and heart-break,—and through it all, though I actually suffer, there, is such an unspeakable lightness and buoyancy, such a lifting up, that even pain is a pleasure. I can't explain it all, unless it is the influence of this mysterious country, lulling and soothing, but powerful and subtle as poison.

My dear girl you say you feel too far away to help me! Now don't you worry about that! If you never wrote me another line, you would help me. Just to know that you are around there, on the other side of the earth, believing in me, loving me, and *approving* of me, means everything. You were right to make me come, and while it cost me my very heart's blood, yet I am learning my lesson as you said I would.

My little ship may never again sail into the harbor of happiness, yet there are sunny seas where soft winds blow, and even if my ship is all by its lonesome, yet it's such a frisky craft, warranted never to sink, no matter what the weather, that it can sail over many seas, touch many lands, and grow rich in experience. And hid away in the locker where no eye save mine may see, are my treasures; your love is one, and nothing can rob me of it.

What you write me of Jack makes me very unhappy. I am not worth his worrying over. Tell him so, Mate. If I could ever care for anybody again in this world, it would be for him, but if an occasional sentiment dares to spring up into my heart, I pull it up by the roots! I would give anything to write to him, but I know it would only bring pain to us both. Be good to him, Mate, I can't bear to think of him being miserable.

I am so tired that I can scarcely keep the tears back. I must write no more.

Hiroshima, November 14, 1902.

I have about fifteen minutes between classes, and I am going to spend them on you. Now who do you suppose has come to the surface again? Little Germany, who was on the steamer coming over. He wasted a great many stamps on me for the first few months after we landed but he got tired of playing solos. He was on his way to Thibet to enter a monastery to study some ancient language. Heaven knows why he wants to know anything more antique than the language he speaks! I don't believe there is any old dusty, forgotten corner of the world that he hasn't poked into.

Well you know the fatal magnetism I exert over fossils! They always turn to me as naturally as needles turn to a

THE LADY OF THE DECORATION

loadstone. This particular mummy was no exception.

I wrote him a formal stately answer, reminding him in gentle reproof that I was a widow (God save the Mark) and that my life was dedicated to my work. It was no use, he bombarded me with letters, with bigger and bigger words and longer and fiercer quotations. In the last one he threatens to come to Hiroshima!

If he does, I am going to shave my eye-brows and black my teeth! He speaks seven languages, and yet he doesn't know the meaning of the one word "no."

Jack used to say that if a man was persistent enough he could win a woman in spite of the Devil. I would like to see him! I mean Jack, not Dutchy nor the Devil.

Hiroshima, Christmas Eve, 1902.

I am in the very thickest of Christmas, and yet such a funny, unreal Christmas, that it does not seem natural at all. Hiroshima is busy decorating for the New Year, and everything is gay with brilliant lanterns, plum blossoms and crimson berries. The little insignificant streets are changed into bowers of sweet smelling ferns and spicy pines, and the bamboo leaves sway to every breeze, while the waxen plum blossoms send out a perfume sweet as violets.

The shop-keepers and their families put on their gayest kimonos and their most enticing smiles and greet you with effusion.

On entering a shop you are asked if your honorable eyes will deign to look upon most unworthy goods. Please will you give this or that a little adoring look? The price? Ah! its price is greatly enhanced since the august foreigner cast honorable eyes upon it. (Which is no joke!) Whether the article is bought or not, the smile, the bow, the compliment are the same. All this time the crowd around the door of the shop has been steadily increasing until daylight is shut out, for everyone is interested in your purchase from the man who hauls the dray up to the highest lady in the land. The shop-keeper is very patient with the crowd until it shuts out the light, then he invites them to carry their useless bodies to the river and throw them in.

Once outside you see another crowd and as curiosity is in the air, you crane your neck and try to get closer. The center of attraction is a man in spotless white cooking bean cake on a little hibachi. The air is cold and crisp, and the smell of the savory bean paste, piping hot, makes you hungry.

Next comes the fish man with a big flat basket on each end of a pole, and offers you a choice lot; long slippery eels, beautiful shrimp, as pink as the sunset, and juicy oysters whose shells have been scrubbed until they are gleaming white. Around the baskets are garlands of paper roses to hide from view the ugly rough edges of the straw.

The candy shops tempt you to the last sen, and the toy shops are a perfect joy. Funny fat Japanese dolls and stuffed rabbits and cross-eyed, tailless cats demand attention.

THE LADY OF THE DECORATION

Perhaps you will see a cheap American doll with blue eyes and yellow hair carefully exhibited under a glass case, and when you are wondering why they treasure this cheap toy, you happen to glance down and catch the worshipping gaze of a wistful, half starved child, and your point of view changes at once and you begin to understand the value of it, and to wish with all your heart that you could put an American dolly in the hands of every little Japanese girl on the Island!

It is getting almost time to open my box and I am right childish over it. It has been here for two days, and I have slipped in a dozen times to look at it and touch it. Oh! Mate, the time has been so long, so cruelly long! I wake myself up in the night some time sobbing. One year and a half behind me, and two and a half ahead! I remember mother telling about the day I started to school, how I came home and said triumphantly, "Just think I've only got ten more years to go to school!"

Poor little duffer! She's still going to school!

Last night I had another mother's meeting for the mothers of the Free Kindergarten. This time I gave a magic lantern show, and I was the showman. The poor, ignorant women sat there bewildered. They had never seen a piano, and many of them had never been close to a foreigner before. I showed them about a hundred slides, explained through an interpreter until I was hoarse, gesticulated and orated to no purpose. They remained silent and stolid. By and by there was a stir, heads were raised, and necks craned.

A sudden interest swept over the room. I followed their gaze and saw on the sheet the picture of Christ toiling up the mountain under the burden of the cross. The story was new and strange to them, but the fact was as old as life itself. At last they had found something that touched their own lives and brought the quick tears of sympathy to their eyes.

I am going to have a meeting every month for them, no matter what else has to go undone.

It is almost time to hang up our stockings. Miss Lessing and Dixie objected at first, but I told them I was either going to be very foolish or very blue, they could take their choice. I have to do something to scare away the ghosts of dead Christmases, so I put on my fool's cap and jingle my bells. When I begin to weaken, I go to the piano and play "Come Ye Disconsolate" to rag time, and it cheers me up wonderfully.

I guess it's just about daylight with you now. Pete is tiptoeing in to make the fires. I can hear him now saying: "Christmas Gif' Mister Sam, Chris'mus Gif' Miss Bettie!" and the children are flying around in their night clothes wild with excitement. Down in the sitting room the stockings make a circle around the room and underneath each is a pile of gifts. I can see the big log fire, and the sparkle of it in the old book-case, and in the long glass between the windows. And in a few minutes here you all come, you uncles and you cousins and you aunts, trooping in with the smallest first. And such laughing, and shouting, and rejoicing! and maybe in the midst of the fun somebody speaks of me, and there's a little hush, and a little longing, then the fun goes on more furiously than ever.

Well even if I am on the wrong side of the earth in body, I am not in spirit, and I reach my arms clear around the world and cry "God bless you, every one."

Hiroshima, March, 1903.

I have a strong conviction that I am going to swear before I get through this letter, for this pen is what I would call, to use unmissionary language, devilish. My! how familiar and wicked that word looks! I've heard so many hymns and so much brotherly and sisterly talk that it seems like meeting an old friend to see it written!

Here it is nearly cherry-blossom time again, and the days and the weeks are slipping away into months before I know it. I am working at full speed and wonder sometimes how I keep up. But I don't dare leave any leisure for heartaches, even when the body is quivering from weariness, and every nerve cries out for rest. I must keep on and on and on, for all too easily the dread memories come creeping back and enfold me until there is no light on any side. From morning until night it is a fight against the tide.

Work is the only thing that keeps me from thinking, and I am determined not to think. I suppose I am as contented here as I could be anywhere. My whole heart is in the kindergarten and the success of it, and maybe the day will come when my work will be all sufficient to satisfy my soul's craving. But it hasn't come yet!

I almost envy some of these good people who can stand in the middle of one of their prayers and touch all four sides. They know what they want and are satisfied when they get it, but I want the moon and the stars and the sun thrown in.

When things seem closing in upon me and everything looks dark, I flee to the woods. I never knew what the trees and the wind and the sky really meant until I came out here and had to make friends of them. I think you have to be by yourself and a bit lonesome before Nature ever begins to whisper her secrets. Can you imagine Philistine Me going out on the hill top to see the sun-rise and going without my supper to see it set? I am even studying the little botany that Jack gave me, though my time and my intellect are equally limited.

And speaking of Jack leads me to remark that there is no necessity for all of you to maintain such an oppressive silence concerning him! Three months ago you wrote me that he was not well, and that he was going south with you and sister. He must be pretty sick to stop work even for a week. I have pictured you sitting with a loaf of bread and a jug of wine beneath the bough quoting poetry at each other to your heart's content.

You say when I come home I can rest on my laurels; no thank you, I want a Morris chair, a pitcher of lemonade, all

THE LADY ᵒᶠᵗʰᵉ DECORATION

the new books and a little darkey to fan me.

Mrs. Heath has asked me to visit her in Vladivostock this summer and I am going if the cholera doesn't get worse. We are so afraid of it that we almost boil the cow before we drink the milk!

Among the delicacies of our menu out here are raw fish, pickled parsnips, sea-weed and bean-paste. As old Charity used to say I've gotten so "acclamitized" I think I could eat a gum shoe.

When they send out my spring box from home, please tell them to put in some fluffy white dresses with elbow sleeves. Then I want lots of pretty ribbons, and a white belt. I saw in the paper that crushed leather was the proper thing. It sounds like something good to eat, but if it's to wear send it along.

My disposition will be everlastingly ruined if I write another line with this pen. Good-bye.

Hiroshima, May, 1903.

Well the catastrophe arrived and we were prisoners for nearly a week. It was not quite cholera but close enough to it to scare us all to death. Both Eve and the apple were young and green, and the combination worked disaster. When the doctor arrived, he shipped Eve off to the inspection hospital, while we were locked up, guarded by five small policemen, and hardly allowed to open our mouths for fear we would swallow a germ. We were fumigated and par-boiled until we felt like steam puddings. Nobody was allowed to go in or out, our vegetables were handed to us in a basket on a bamboo pole over the wall. We tied notes to bricks and flung them to our neighbors on the outside. Thank Heaven, the servants were locked in too. Every day a little man with lots of brass buttons and a big voice came and asked anxiously after our honorable insides.

I used every inducement to get them to let me go out for exercise. I fixed a tray with my prettiest cups and sent a pot of steaming coffee and a plate of cake out to the lodge house. Word came back, "We are not permitted to drink or taste food in an infected house." Then I tried them on button-hole bouquets, and when that failed, I got desperate, and announced that I was subject to fits, unless I got regular outside exercise every day. That fetched them and they gave the foreign teachers permission to walk in the country for half an hour provided we did not speak to any one.

Eve was up and having a good time before the school gates were opened.

While a prisoner, I did all sorts of odd jobs, patched, mended, darned, wrote letters, and chopped down two trees. The latter was a little out of my line, but the trees were eaten up with caterpillars, and as I could not get anybody to cut them down, I sallied forth and did it myself. My chef stood by and admired the job, but he would not assist for fear he would unwittingly murder one of his ancestors!

You would certainly laugh to see me keeping house with a cook book, a grocery book and a dictionary. The other day I gave directions for poached eggs, and the maid served them in a huge pan full of water.

There are one hundred and twenty-five yellow kids waiting for me so I must hurry away.

Vladivostock, Siberia, July, 1903.

I didn't mean that it should be so long a time before I wrote you, but the closing of school, the Commencement, and the getting ready to come up here about finished me. You remember the old darkey song, "Wisht I was in Heaben, settin' down"? Well that was my one ambition and I about realized it when I got up here to Mrs. Heath's and she put me in a hammock in a quiet corner of the porch and made me keep blissfully still for two whole days.

The air is just as bracing, the hills are just as green, and the lights and shadows dance over the harbor just as of old. We have tennis, golf, picnics, sails, and constant jollification, but I don't seem to enjoy it all as I did last summer. It isn't altogether homesickness, though that is chronic, it is a constant longing for I don't know what.

Viewed impersonally, the world is a rattling good show, but instead of smiling at it from the front row in the dress circle, I get to be one of the performers every time.

We have been greatly interested in watching the Russians build a fort on one of their islands near here. They insist there will be no war and at the same time they are mining the harbor and building forts day and night. The minute it is dark the searchlights are kept busy sweeping the harbor in search of something not strictly Russian. I hope I will get back as safely as I got here.

Did I tell you that I stopped over two days in Korea? I had often heard of the Jumping Off Place, but I never expected to actually see it! The people live in the most awful little mud houses, and their poverty is appalling. No streets, no roads, no anything save a fog of melancholy that seems to envelop everything. The terrible helplessness of the people, their ignorance, and isolation are terrible.

The box from home was more than satisfactory. I have thoroughly enjoyed wearing all the pretty things. The hat sister sent was about the size of a turn-table; a strong hat pin and a slight breeze will be all I need to travel to No Man's Land. Sister says it's *moderate*, save the mark! but it really is becoming and when I get it on, my face looks like a pink moon emerging from a fleecy black cloud. I had to practice wearing it in private until I learned to balance it properly.

I shall stay up here through July and then I am thinking of going to Shanghai with Mrs. Heath's sister, who lives there. I am very fond of her, and I know I would have a good time. I feel a little like a subscription list, being passed around this way, but I simply *have* to keep going every minute when I am not at work.

They are calling up to me from the tennis court so I must stop for the present.

SHANGHAI, CHINA, August, 1903.

The mail goes out this morning and I am determined to get this letter written if I break up a dozen parties. As you see, I am in Shanghai, this wonderful big understudy for Chicago, which seems about as incongruous in its surroundings as a silk hat on a haystack! There are beautiful boulevards, immense houses, splendid public gardens, all hedged in by a yellow mass of orientals.

Every nationality is represented here, and people meet, mingle, and separate in an ever changing throng. At every corner stands a tall majestic Sikh, with head bound in yards of crimson cloth, directing the movements of the crowd. Down the street comes a regiment of English soldiers, so big and determined that one well understands their victories. The ubiquitous Russian makes himself known at every turn, silent and grave, but in his simplest dealings as merciless and greedy as the country he represents. Frenchmen and Germans, and best of all, the unquenchable American, join in the panorama, and the result is something that one does not see anywhere else on the globe. I guess if my dear brethren knew of the theatre parties, dinners and dances I was going to, they would think I was on a toboggan slide for the lower regions! I am not though. I am simply getting a good swing to the pendulum so that I can go back to "the field," and the baby organs and the hymn-singing with better grace. It is very funny, but do you know that for a *steady diet* I can stand the saints much better than I can the sinners!

My friends the Carters live right on the Bund facing the water. They keep lots of horses and many servants, and live in a luxury that only the East can offer. Every morning before I am up a slippery Chinese, all done up in livery, comes to my room and solemnly announces: "Missy bath allee ready, nice morning, good-bye." From that time on I am scarcely allowed to carry my pocket handkerchief!

The roads about here are perfect, and we drive for hours past big country houses, all built in English fashion. There is one grewsome feature in the landscape, however, and that is the Chinese graves. In the fields, in the back and front yards, on the highways, any bare space that is large enough to set a box and cover it with a little earth, serves as a burying ground.

I am interested in it all, and enjoying it in a way, but, Mate, there is no use fibbing to you, there is a restlessness in my heart that sometimes almost drives me crazy. There is nothing under God's sun that can repay a woman for the loss of love and home. It's all right to love humanity, but I was born a specialist. The past is torn out by the roots but the awful emptiness remains. I am not grieving over what has been, but what isn't. That last sentence sounds malarial, I am going right upstairs to take a quinine pill.

Soochow, August, 1903.

Well, Mate, this is the first letter I have really written you from China. Shanghai doesn't count. Soochow is the real article. The unspeakable quantity and quality of dirt surpasses anything I have ever imagined. Dirt and babies, there are millions of babies, under your feet, around your heels, every nook and corner full of babies.

From Shanghai to Soochow is only a one night trip, and as I had an invitation to come up for over Sunday, I decided to take advantage of it. You would have to see the boat I came in to appreciate it. They call it a house-boat, but it is built on a pattern that is new to me. In the lower part are rooms, each of which is supplied with a board on which you are supposed to sleep. Each passenger carries his own bedding and food. In the upper part of the boat is a sort of loft just high enough for a man to sit up, and in it are crowded hundreds of the common people. A launch tows seven or eight of these house-boats at a time. I will not ask you to even imagine the condition of them; I had to stand it because I was there, but you are not.

It was just at sunset when we left Shanghai, and I got as far away from the crowd as I could and tried to forget my unsavory surroundings. The sails of thousands of Chinese vessels loomed black and big against the red sky as they floated silently by without a ripple. In the dim light, I read on the prow of a bulky schooner, " 'The Mary', Boston, U.S.A." Do you know how my heart leapt out to "The Mary, Boston, U.S.A."? It was the one thing in all that vast, unfamiliar world that spoke my tongue.

When I went to my room, I found that a nice little Chinese girl in a long sack coat and shiny black trousers was to share it with me. I must confess that I was relieved for I was lonesome and a bit nervous, and when I discovered that she knew a little English I could have hugged her. We spread our cold supper on the top of my dress suit case, put our one candle in the center, and proceeded to feast. Little Miss Izy was not as shy as she looked, and what she lacked in vocabulary she made up in enthusiasm. We got into a gale of laughter over our efforts to understand each other, and she was as curious about my costume as I was about hers. She watched me undress with unfeigned amusement, following the lengthy process carefully, then she rose, untied a string, stepped out of her coat and trousers, stood for a moment in a white suit made exactly like her outer garments, then gaily kicked off her tiny slippers and rolled over in bed. I don't know if this is a universal custom in China, but at any rate, little Miss Izy will never be like the old lady, who committed suicide because she was so tired of buttoning and unbuttoning.

The next morning we were in Soochow, at least outside of the city wall. They say the wall is over two thousand years old and it certainly looks it, and the spaces on top left for the guns to point through make it look as if it had lost most of its teeth. Things are so old in this place, Mate, that I feel as if I had just been born! I have nearly ran my legs off sightseeing; big pagodas and little pagodas, Mamma Buddhas and Papa Buddhas, and baby Buddhas, all of whom look exactly like their first cousins in Japan.

Soochow is just a collection of narrow alley-ways over which the house tops meet, and through which the people swarm by the millions, sellers crying their wares, merchants urging patronage, children screaming, beggars displaying their infirmities, and through it all coolies carrying sedan chairs scattering the crowd before them.

In many of the temples, the priests hang wind bells to frighten the evil spirits away. I think it is a needless precaution, for it would only be a feeble-minded spirit that would ever want to return to China once it had gotten away!

HIROSHIMA, October, 1903.

In harness again and glad of it. I've opened the third kindergarten with the money from home; it's only a little one, eighteen children in all, and there were seventy-five applicants, but it is a beginning. You ought to see the mothers crowding around, begging and pleading for their children to be taken in, and the little tots weep and wail when they have to go home. I feel to-day as if I would almost resort to highway robbery to get money enough to carry on this work!

My training class is just as interesting as it can be. When the girls came to me two years ago they were in the Third Reader. With two exceptions, I have given them everything that was included in my own course at home, and taught them English besides. They are very ambitious, and what do you suppose is their chief aim in life? To study until they know as much as I do! Oh! Mate, it makes me want to hide my head in shame, when I think of all the opportunities I wasted. You know only too well what a miserable little rubbish pile of learning I possess, but what you *don't* know is how I have studied and toiled and burned the midnight tallow in trying to work over those old odds and ends into something useful for my girls. If they have made such progress under a superficial, shallow-pated thing like me, what *would* they have done under a woman with brains?

I wish you could look in on me to-night sitting here surrounded by all my household goods. The room is bright and cozy, and just at present I have a room-mate. It is a little sick girl from the training class, whom I have taken care of since I came back. She belongs to a very poor family down in the country, her mother is dead, and her home life is very unhappy. She nearly breaks her heart crying when we speak of sending her home, and begs me to help her get well so she can go on with her studies.

Of course she is a great care, but I get up a little earlier and go to bed a little later, and so manage to get it all in.

We are getting quite stirred up over the war clouds that are hanging over this little water-color country. Savage old Russia is doing a lot of bullying, and the Japanese are not going to stand much more. They are drilling and marching and soldiering now for all they are worth. From Kuri, the naval station, we can hear the thunder of the guns which are in constant practice. Out on the parade grounds, in the barracks, on every country road preparation is going on. Officers high in rank and from the Emperor's guard are here reviewing the troops. Those who know say a crash is bound to come. So if you hear of me in a red cross uniform at the front, you needn't be surprised.

HIROSHIMA, November, 1903.

My dear old Mate:

I am just tired enough to-night to fold my hands, and turn up my toes and say "Enough." If overcoming difficulties makes character, then I will have as many characters as the Chinese alphabet by the time I get through. The bothers meet me when the girl makes the fire in the morning and puts the ashes in the grate instead of the coal, and they keep right along with me all day until I go to bed at night and find the sheet under the mattress and the pillows at the foot.

It wouldn't be near so hard if I could charge around, and

let off a little of my wrath, but no, I must be nice and sweet and polite and *never* forget that I am an Example.

Have you ever seen these dolls that have a weight in them, so that you can push them over and they stand right up again? Well I have a large one and her name is Susie Damn. When things reach the limit of endurance, I take it out on Susie Damn. I box her jaws and knock her over, and up she comes every time with such a pleasant smile that I get in a good humor again.

What is the matter with you at home? Why don't you write to me? I used to get ten and twelve letters every mail, and now if I get one I am ready to cry for joy. Because I am busy does not mean that I haven't time to be lonely. Why, Mate, you can never know what loneliness means until you are entirely away from everything you love. I have tried to be brave but I haven't always made a grand success of it. What I have suffered—well don't let me talk about it. As Little Germany says, to live is to love, and to love is to suffer. And yet it is for that love we are ready to suffer and die, and without it life is a blank, a sail without a wind, a frame without the picture!

Now to-morrow I may get one of your big letters, and you will tell me how grand I am, and how my soul is developing, etc., and I'll get such a stiff upper lip that my front teeth will be in danger. It takes a stiff upper lip, and a stiff conscience, and a stiff everything else to keep going out here!

From the foregoing outburst you probably think I am

pale and dejected. "No, on the contrary," as the seasick Frenchman said when asked if he had dined. I am hale and hearty, and I never had as much color in my life. The work is booming, and I have all sorts of things to be thankful for.

Our little household has been very much upset this week by the death of our cook. The funeral took place last night at seven o'clock from the lodge house at the gate. The shadows made on the paper screens as they prepared him for burial, told an uncanny story. The lack of delicacy, the coarseness, the total disregard for the dignity of death were all pictured on the doors. I stood in the chapel and watched with a sick heart. After they had crowded the poor old body into a sitting position in a sort of square tub, they brought it out to the coolies who were to carry it to the temple, and afterward to the crematory. The lanterns flickered with an unsteady light, making grotesque figures that seemed to dance in fiendish glee on the grass. The men laughed and chattered, and at last shouldered their burden and trotted off as merrily as if they were going to a matsuri. I never before felt the cruelty of heathenism so keenly. No punishment in the next world can equal the things they miss in this life by a lack of belief in a personal God.

It must be very beautiful at home about this time. The beech trees are all green and gold, and the maples are blazing. I am thinking too about the shadows on the old ice-house. I know every one of them by heart, and they often come to haunt me as do many other shadows of the sad, sad past.

Hiroshima, December, 1903.

God bless you honey, I've got a holiday and I've sworn vengeance on anyone who comes to my door until I have written my Christmas letters. I wish I was a doctor and a trained nurse, and a scholar, a magician, a philosopher and a saint all combined. I need them in my business.

I have spent this merry Christmas season, chasing from pillow to post with bandages, hot water bags, poultices and bottles. We have had a regular hospital. All the Christmas money I had saved to buy presents for home went in Cod Liver Oil, and Miss Lessing, bless her soul, is doing without a coat for the same purpose. When you see a girl struggling for what little education she can get, and know what sacrifices are being made for it, you just hate your frumpery old finery, and you want to convert everything you possess into cash to help her. All the teachers are doing without fires in their rooms this winter, and it is rather chillsome to go to bed cold and wake up next morning in the same condition. When I get home to a furnace-heated house and have cream in my coffee, I shall feel too dissipated to be respectable!

We have not been able to get a new cook since our old one died, and the fact must have gotten abroad, for all the floating brethren and sisters in Japan have been to see us! Y.M.C.A.'s, W.C.T.U.'s, A.W.B.M.'s and X.Y.Z.'s have sifted in, and we have to sit up and be Marthas and Marys all at the same time!

Sometimes I want to get my hat and run and run until I get to another planet. But I am not made of the stuff that runs, and I have the satisfaction of knowing that I have stuck to my post. If sacrificing self, and knocking longings in the head, and smashing heart-aches right and left, do not pass me through the Golden Gate, then I'll sue Peter for damages.

It's snowing to-day, but the old Earth is making about as poor a bluff at being Christmasy as I am. The leaves are all on the trees, many flowers are in bloom, and the scarlet geraniums are warm enough to melt the snow flakes.

My big box has arrived and I am keeping it until tomorrow. I go out and sit on it every little while to keep cheered up. This is my third Christmas from home, one more and then—!

There has been too much sickness to make much of the holiday, but I have rigged up a fish pond for the kindergarten children, and each kiddie will have a present that cost one-fourth of a cent! I wish I had a hundred dollars to spend on them!

To-night when the lights are out, my little sick girl's stocking will hang on one bed post, and mine on the other. I don't believe Santa Claus will have the heart to pass us by, do you?

HIROSHIMA, January, 1904.

Here it is January and I am just thanking you dear ones for my beautiful Christmas box. As you probably guessed, Mate, our Christmas was not exactly hilarious. The winter has been a hard one, the prospect of war has sent the price of provisions out of sight, the sick girls in the school have needed medicine and fires, so altogether Miss Lessing, Miss Dixon and I have had to do considerable tugging at the ends to get them to meet. None of us have bought a stitch of new clothing this winter, so when our boxes came, we were positively dazed by all the grandeur.

They arrived late at night and we got out of bed to open them. The first thing I struck was a very crumpled little paper doll, with baby Bess' name printed in topsy-turvy letters on the back. For the next five minutes I was kept busy swallowing the lumps that came in my throat, but Dixie had some peppermint candy out of her box, the first I had seen since I had left home, so I put on my lovely new beaver hat, which with my low-necked gown and red slippers was particularly chic, and I sat on the floor and ate candy. It—the hat and the candy too, went a long way towards restoring my equanimity, but I didn't dare look at that paper doll again that night!

You ask if I mind wearing that beautiful crêpe de chine which is not becoming to you? Well, Mate, I suppose there was a day when I would have scorned anybody's cast-off clothes, but I pledge you my word a queen in her coronation robes never felt half so grand as I feel in that dress! Somehow I seem to assume some of your personality, I look tall and graceful and dignified, and I try to imagine how it feels to be good and intellectual, and fascinating, and besides I have the satisfaction of knowing that I am rather becoming to the dress myself! It fits without a wrinkle and next summer with my big black hat,—! Well, if Little Germany sees me, there will be something doing!

I must tell you an experience I had the other day. Miss Lessing and I were coming back on the train from Miyajima and sitting opposite to us was an old couple who very soon told us that they had never seen foreigners before. They were as guileless as children, and presently the old man came over and asked if he might look at my jacket. I had no objections, so he put his hands lightly on my shoulders and turned me around for inspection. "But," he said to Miss Lessing in Japanese, "how does she get into it?" I took it off to show him and in so doing revealed fresh wonders. He returned to his wife, and after a long consultation, and many inquiring looks, he came back. He said he knew he was a great trouble, but I was most honorably kind, and would I tell him why I wore a piece of leather about my waist, and would I please remove my dress and show them how I put it on? He was distinctly disappointed when I declined, but he managed to get in one more question and that was if we slept in our hats. When he got off, he assured us that he had never seen anything so interesting in his life, and he would have great things to tell the people of his village.

There isn't a place you go, or a thing you do out here that doesn't afford some kind of amusement.

The first glamour of the country has gotten dimmed a bit, not that the interest has waned for a moment, but I have come to see that the beauty and picturesqueness are largely on the surface. If ever I have to distribute tracts in another world, I am going to wrap a piece of soap in every one, for I am more and more convinced that the surest way to heaven for the heathen is the Soapy Way.

During the holidays I tried to study up a little and add a drop or two to that gray matter that is supposed to be floating around in my brain. But as a girl said of a child in Kindergarten, "my intelligence was not working." Putting Psychology into easy terms, stopping to explain things I do not understand very well myself, struggling through the medium of a strange language, and trying to occidentalize the oriental mind has been a stiff proposition for one whose learning was never her long suit! When I come home I may be nothing but a giggly, childishly happy old lady, who doesn't care a rap whether her skin fits or not.

The prospect of war is getting more and more serious. Out in the Inland Sea, the war ships are hastening here and there on all sorts of secret missions. I hope with all my heart there will not be war, but if there is, I hope Japan will wipe Russia right off the map!

THE LADY ᴼᶠ ᵀᴴᴱ DECORATION

Hiroshima, February, 1904.

Dear old Mate:

I am breathless! For three weeks I have had a chase up hill and down dale, to the top of pine clad mountains, into the misty shadows of the deep valleys, up and down the silvery river, to and fro on the frosty road. For why! All because I had lost my "poise," that treasured possession which you said I was to hang on to as I do to my front teeth and my hair. So when I found it was gone, I started in full pursuit. Never a sight of its coat tails did I catch until Sunday, when I gave up the race and sat me down to fight out the old fight of rebellion, and kicking against the pricks.

It was a perfect day, the plum trees were white with blossom, the spice bushes heavy with fragrance, the river dancing for joy, and the whole earth springing into new, tender life. A saucy little bird sat on an old stone lantern, and sang straight at me. He told me I was a whiney young person, that it was lots more fun to catch worms and fly around in the sunshine than it was to sit in the house and mope. He actually laughed at me, and I seized my hat and lit out after him, and when I came home I found I had caught my "poise."

To-day in class I asked my girls what "happiness" meant. One new girl looked up timidly and said, "Sensei, I sink him just mean *you*." I felt like a hypocrite, but it pleased me to know that on the outside at least I kept shiny.

I tell you if I don't find my real self out here, if I don't see my own soul in all its bareness and weakness then I will never see it. At home hedged in by conventionality, custom, and the hundred little interests of our daily life, we have small chance to see ourselves as we really are, but in a foreign land stripped bare of everything in the world save *self*, in a loneliness as great sometimes as the grave, face to face with new conditions, new demands, we have ample chance to take our own measurement. I cannot say that the result obtained is calculated to make one conceited!

I fit into this life out here, like a square peg in a round hole. I am not consecrated, I was never "*called* to the foreign field," I love the world and the flesh even if I don't care especially for the devil, I don't believe the Lord makes the cook steal so I may be more patient, and I don't pray for wisdom in selecting a new pair of shoes. When my position becomes unbearable, I invariably face the matter frankly and remind myself that if it is hard on the peg, it is just as hard on the hole, and that if they can stand it I guess I can!

You ask about my reading. Yes, I read every spare minute I can get, before breakfast, on my way to classes, and after I go to bed. Somebody at home sends me the magazines regularly and I keep them going for months.

By the way I wish you would write and tell me just exactly how Jack is. You said he was working too hard and that he looked all fagged out. Wasn't it exactly like him to back out of going South on account of his conscience? He would laugh at us for saying it was that, but it was. He may be unreligious, and scoff at churches and all that, but he has the most rigid, cast-iron, inelastic conscience that I ever came across. I wish he would take a rest. You see out here, so far away from you all, I can't help worrying when any of you are the least bit sick. Jack has been on my mind for days. Don't tell him that I asked you to, but won't you get him to go away? He would curl his hair if you asked him to.

Preparations for war are still in progress and it makes a fellow pretty shivery to see it coming closer and closer. Hiroshima will be the center of military movements and of course under military law. It will affect us only as to the restrictions put on our walks and places we can go. With the city so full of strange soldiers, I don't suppose we will want to go much. Two big war ships, which Japan has just bought from Chile are on their way from Shanghai. Regiment after regiment has poured into Hiroshima and embarked again for Corea. I am terribly thrilled over it all, and the Japanese watch my enthusiasm with their non-committal eyes and never say a word!

My poor little sick girl grows weaker all the time. She is a constant care and anxiety, but she has no money and I cannot send her back to her wretched home. The teachers think I am very foolish to let the thing run on, and I suppose I am. She can never be any better, and she may live this way for months. But when she clings to me with her frail hands and declares she is better and will soon get well if I will only let her stay with me, my heart fails me. I have patched up an old steamer chair for her, and made a window garden, and tried to make the room as bright as possible. She has to stay by herself nearly all day, but she is so patient and gentle that I never hear a complaint. This morning she pressed my hand to her breast and said wistfully, "Sensei, it makes sorry to play all the time with the health."

Miss Lessing tried to get her in the hospital but they will not take incurables.

Somehow Jack's hospital scheme doesn't seem as foolish as it did. If there are other children in the world as friendless and dependent as this one, then making a permanent home for them would be worth all the great careers in the world.

HIROSHIMA, March, 1904.

My Best Girl:

Don't I wish you were here to share all these thrills with me! War is actually in progress, and if you could see me hanging out of the window at midnight yelling for a special, then chasing madly around to get someone to translate it for me, see me dancing in fiendish glee at every victory won by this brave little country, you would conclude that I am just as young as I used to be. I tell you I couldn't be prouder of my own country! Just think of plucky little old Japan winning three battles from those big, brutal, conceited Russians. Why I just want to run and hug the Emperor!

And the school girls! Why their placid faces are positively glorified by the fire of patriotism. Once a week a trained nurse comes to give talks on nursing, and if I go into any corner afterward, I find a group of girls practising all kinds of bandaging. Even the demurest little maiden cherishes the hope that some fate may send her to the battle-field, or that in some way she may be permitted to serve her country.

I am afraid I am not very strict about talking in class these days, but, somehow, courage, nobility, and self-sacrifice seem just as worthy of attention as "motor ideas," and "apperceptions."

A British guest who hates everything Japanese says my enthusiasm "is quite annoying, you know," but, dear me, I don't mind him. What could you expect of a person who eats pie with a spoon? Why my enthusiasm is just cutting its eye-teeth! The whole country is a-thrill, and even a wooden Indian would get excited.

Every afternoon we walk down on the sea wall and watch the preparations going on for a long siege. Hundreds of big ships fill the harbor to say nothing of the small ones, and there are thousands of coolies working like mad. I could tell you many interesting things, but I am afraid of the censor. If he deciphers all my letters home, he will probably have nervous prostration by the time the war is over.

Many of the war ships are coaled by women who carry heavy baskets on each end of a pole swung across the shoulder, and invariably a baby on their backs. It is something terrible the way the women work, often pulling loads that would require a horse at home. They go plodding past us on the road, dressed as men, mouth open, eyes straining, all intelligence and interest gone from their faces.

One day as Miss Lessing and I were resting by the roadside, one of these women stopped for breath just in front of us. She was pushing a heavy cart and her poor old body was trembling from the strain. Her legs were bare, and her feet were cut by the stones. There was absolute stolidity in her weather-beaten face, and the hands that lighted her pipe were gnarled and black. Miss Lessing has a perfect genius for getting at people, I think it is her good kind face through which her soul shines. She asked the old woman if she was very tired. The woman looked up, as if seeing us for the first time and nodded her head. Then a queer look came into her face and she asked Miss Lessing if we were the kind of people who had a new God. Miss Lessing told her we were Christians. With a wistfulness that I have never seen except in the eyes of a dog, she said, "If I paid your God with offering and prayers, do you think he would make my work easier? I am so tired!" Miss Lessing made her sit down by her on the grass, and talked to her in Japanese about the new God who did not take any pay for his help, and who could put something in her heart that would give her strength to bear any burden. I could not understand much of what they said but I had a little prayer-meeting all by myself.

Hiroshima, April, 1904.

Yesterday the American mail came after a three weeks' delay. None of us were good for anything the rest of the day. Twenty letters and fifty-two papers for me! Do you wonder that I almost danced a hole in the parlor rug?

The home news was all so bright and cheery, and your letter was such a bunch of comfort that I felt like a two year old. It was exactly like you to think out that little farm party and get Jack into it as a matter of accommodation to you. I followed everything you did, with the keenest interest, from the all-day tramps in the woods, to the cozy evenings around the log fire. I can see old Jack now, at first bored to death but resolved to die if need be on the altar of friendship, gradually warming up as he always does out of doors, and ending up by being the life of the party. He once told me that social success is the infinite capacity for being bored. I know the little outing did him a world of good, and you are all the trumps in the deck as usual.

Who is the Dr. Leet that was in the party? I remember dancing a cotillon with a very good looking youth of that name in the prehistoric ages. He was a senior at Yale, very rich and very good looking. I wore his fraternity pin over my heart for a whole week afterward.

We have been having great fun over the American accounts of the war. Through the newspapers we learn the most marvelous things about Japan and her people. Large cities are unblushingly moved from the coast to an island in the Inland Sea, troops are passported from places which have no harbor, and the people are credited with unheard of customs.

We are still in the midst of stirring times. The city is overflowing with troops, and we are hemmed in on every side by soldiers. Of course foreign women are very curious to them, and they often follow us and make funny comments, but we have never yet had a single rudeness shown us. In all the thousands of soldiers stationed here, I have only seen two who were tipsy, and they were mildly hilarious from saki. There is perfect order and discipline, and after nine o'clock at night the streets are as quiet as a mountain village.

The other night, five of the soldiers, mere boys, donned citizens' dress and went out for a lark. At roll-call they were missing and a guard was sent to search for them. When found, they resisted arrest and three minutes after they all answered the roll-call in another world.

And yet although the discipline is so severe, the men seem a contented and happy lot. They stroll along the roads when off duty hand in hand like school girls, and laugh and chatter as if life were a big holiday. But when the time comes to go to the front, they don their gay little uniforms, and march just as joyfully away to give the last drop of their blood for their Emperor.

I tell you, Mate, I want to get out in the street and cheer every regiment that passes! No drum, no fife, no inspiring music to stir their blood and strengthen their courage, nothing but the unvarying monotony of the four note trumpets. They don't need music to make them go. They are perfect little machines whose motive power is a patriotism so absolute, so complete, that it makes death on the battle-field an honor worthy of deification.

I look out into the play-ground, and every boy down to the smallest baby in the kindergarten is armed with a bamboo gun. Such drilling and marching, and attacking of forts you have never seen. That the enemy is nothing more than sticks stuck at all angles matters little. An enemy there must be, and the worst boy in Japan would die before he would even *play* at being a Russian! If Kuropatkin could see just one of these awful onslaughts, he would run up the white flag and hie himself to safety. So you see we are well guarded and with quiet little soldiers on the outside, and very noisy and fierce little soldiers on the inside, we fear no invasion of our peaceful compound.

On my walks around the barracks, I often pass the cook house, and watch the food being carried to the mess room. The rice buckets, about the size of our water buckets, are put on a pole in groups of six or eight and carried on the shoulders of two men. There is a line about a square long of these buckets, and then another long line follows with trays of soup bowls. Tea is not as a rule drunk with the meals, but after the last grain of rice has been chased from the slippery sides of the bowl, hot water is poured in and sipped with loud appreciation.

Last Sunday afternoon we had to entertain ten officers of high rank, and it proved a regular lark. Their English and our Japanese got fatally twisted. One man took great pride in showing me how much too big his clothes were, giving him ample opportunity to put on several suits of underwear in cold weather; he said "Many cloth dese trusers hab, no fit like 'Merican." They were delighted with all our foreign possessions, and inspected everything minutely. On leaving, one officer bowed low, and assured me that he would never see me on earth again, but he hoped he would see me in heaven *first*!

The breezes from China waft an occasional despairing epistle from Little Germany, but they find me as cold as a snow bank on the north side of a mountain. The sun that melts my heart will have to rise in the west, and get up early at that.

Hiroshima, May, 1904.

Well commencement is over and my first class is graduated. Now if you have ever heard of anything more ridiculous than that please cable me! If you could have seen me standing on the platform dealing out diplomas, you would

THE LADY OF THE DECORATION

have been highly edified.

Last night I gave the class a dinner. There were fourteen girls, only two of whom had ever been at a foreign table before. At first they were terribly embarrassed, but before long they warmed up to the occasion and got terribly tickled over their awkwardness. I was afraid they would knock their teeth out with the knives and forks, and the feat of getting soup from the spoon to the mouth proved so difficult that I let them drink it from the bowl. Sitting in chairs was as hard for them as sitting on the floor for me, so between the courses we had a kind of cake walk.

Next week school begins again, and I start three new kindergartens, making seven over which I have supervision. I am so pleased over the progress of my work that I don't know what to do. Not that I don't realize my limitations, heaven knows I do. Imagine my efforts at teaching the training class psychology! The other day we were struggling with the subject of reflex action, and one of the girls handed in this definition as she had understood it from me! "Reflex action is of a activity nervous. It is sometimes the don't understand of what it is doing and stops many messages to the brain and sends the motion to the legs." What little knowledge I start with gets cross-eyed before I get through.

The Japanese can twist the English language into some of the strangest knots that you ever saw. There is a sign quite near here that reads "Cows milk and Retailed."

Since writing you last, I have sent my little sick girl

home. It almost broke us all up, but she couldn't stay here alone during the summer and there was nobody to take care of her. I write to her every week and try to keep her cheered up, but for such as she there is only one release and that is death.

If Jack's hospital ever materializes, I am going to offer my services as a nurse. This poor child's plight has taken such a hold upon me that I long to do something for all the sick waifs in creation.

HIROSHIMA, June, 1904.

It is Sunday afternoon, and your Foreign Missionary Kindergarten Teacher, instead of trudging off to Sunday School with the other teachers, is recklessly sitting in dressing gown and slippers with her golden hair hanging down her hack, writing letters home. After teaching all week, and listening for two hours to a Japanese sermon Sunday morning, I cross my fingers on teaching Sunday School in the afternoon.

This past week I have been trying to practice the simple life. It was a good time for we had spring cleaning, five guests, daily prayer-meetings, two new cooks, and an earthquake. I think by the time I get through, I'll be qualified to run a government on some small Pacific Isle.

The whole city is in confusion, ninety thousand soldiers are here now, and eighty thousand more are expected this

THE LADY OF THE DECORATION

week. Every house-holder must take as many as he can accommodate, and the strain on the people is heavy.

We heard yesterday of the terrible disaster to the troops that left here on the 13th, three transports were sunk by the Russians. Five hundred of the wounded from South Hill battle have been brought here, and whenever I go out, I see long lines of stretchers and covered ambulances bringing in more men. It is intolerable to be near so much suffering and not to be able to relieve it. We are all so worked up with pity and indignation, and sympathy that we hardly dare talk about the war.

Summer vacation will soon be here and I am planning a wild career of self indulgence. I am going to Karuizawa, where I can get cooled off and rested and invite my soul to my heart's content.

For two mortal weeks the rain has poured in torrents. The rainy season out here isn't any of your nice polite little shower-a-day affairs, it is just one interminable downpour, until the old earth is spanked into submission. I can't even remember how sunshine looks, and my spirits are mildewed and my courage is mouldy.

To add to the discomfort, we are besieged by mosquitoes. They are the big ferocious kind that carry off a finger at a time. I heard of one missionary down in the country, who was so bothered one night that he hung his trousers to the ceiling, and put his head in one leg, and made his wife put her head in the other, while the rest of the garment served as a breathing tube!

It has been nearly a year since I was out of Hiroshima, a year of such ups and downs that I feel as if I had been digging out my salvation with a pick-ax.

Not that I do not enjoy the struggle; real life with all its knocks and bumps, its joys and sorrows, is vastly preferable to a passive existence of indolence. Only occasionally I look forward to the time when I shall be an angel frivoling in the eternal blue! Just think of being reduced to a nice little curly head and a pair of wings! That's the kind of angel I am going to be. With no legs to ache, and no heart to break—but dear me it is more than likely that I will get rheumatism in my wings!

If ever I do get to heaven, it will be on your ladder, Mate. You have coaxed me up with confidence and praise, you have steadied me with ethical culture books, and essays, and sermons. You have gotten me so far up (for me), that I am afraid to look down. I shrink with a mighty shrivel when I think of disappointing you in any way, and I expand almost to bursting when I think of justifying your belief in me.

KARUIZAWA, July, 1904.

Here I am comfortably established in the most curious sort of double-barreled house you ever saw. The front part is all Japanese and faces on one street, and the back part is foreign and faces on another street a square away. The two are connected by a covered walk which passes over a mill race. In the floor of the walk just over the water is a trap door, and look out when I will I can see the Japanese stopping to take a bath in this little opening.

I have a nice big room and so much service thrown in that it embarrasses me. When I come in, in the evening, three little maids escort me to my room, one fixes the mosquito bar, one gets my gown, and one helps to undress me. When they have done all they can think of, they get in a row, all bow together, then pitter patter away.

The clerk has to make out the menus and as his English is limited, he calls upon me very often to help him. Yesterday he came with only one entry and that was "Corns on the ear." In return for my assistance he always announces my bath, and escorts me to the bath room carrying my sponge and towels.

As to Karuizawa, it has a summer population of about four hundred, three hundred and ninety-nine of whom are missionaries. Let us all unite in singing "Blest be the tie that binds."

Everybody at our table is in the mission field. A long-nosed young preacher who sits opposite me looks as if he had spent all his life in some kind of a field. He has a terrible attack of religion; I never saw anybody take it any harder. He told me that he was engaged to be married and for three days he had been consulting the Lord about what kind of a ring he should buy!

Sunday I went to church and heard my first English

sermon in two years. We met in a rough little shanty, built in a cluster of pines, and almost every nation was represented. A young English clergyman read the service, and afterward said a few words about sacrifice. He was simple and sincere, and his deep voice trembled with earnestness as he declared that sacrifice was the only true road to happiness, sacrifice of ourselves, our wishes and desires, for the good and the progress of others. And suddenly all the feeling in me got on a rampage and I wanted to get up and say that it was true, that I knew it was true, that the most miserable, pitiful, smashed-up life, could blossom again if it would only blossom for others. I walked home in a sort of ecstasy and at dinner the long-nosed young preacher said: " 'T was a pity we couldn't have regular preaching, there was such a peart lot at meeting." This is certainly a good place to study people's eccentricities, their foibles and follies, to hear them preach and see them *not* practice!

One more year and I will be home. Something almost stops in my heart as I write it! Of course I am glad you are going abroad in the spring, you have been living on the prospect of seeing Italy all your life. Only, Mate, I am selfish enough to want you back by the time I get home. It would take just one perfect hour of seeing you all together once more to banish the loneliness of all these years!

I am glad Jack and Dr. Leet have struck up such a friendship. Jack uses about the same care in selecting a friend that most men do in selecting a wife. Tell Dr. Leet that I am glad he found me in a pigeon hole of his memory, but that I am a long way from being "the blue-eyed bunch of mischief" he describes. I wish you would tell him that I am slender, pale, and pensive with a glamour of romance and mystery hovering about me; that is the way I would like to be.

I knew you could get Jack out of his rut if you tried. The Browning evenings must be highly diverting, I can imagine you reading a few lines for him to expound, then him reading a few for you to explain, then both gazing into space with "the infinite cry of finite hearts that yearn!"

Dear loyal old Jack! How memories stab me as I think of him. It seems impossible to think of him as other than well and strong and self reliant. What happy, happy days I have spent with him! They seem to stand out to-night in one great white spot of cheerfulness. When the days were the darkest and I couldn't see one inch ahead, Jack would happen along with a funny story or a joke, would pretend not to see what was going on, but do some little kindness that would brighten the way a bit. What a mixture he is of tenderness, and brusqueness, of common sense and poetry, of fun and seriousness! I think you and I are the only ones in the world who quite understand his heights and depths. He says even I don't.

KARUIZAWA, July, 1904.

Since writing you I have had the pleasure of looking six

hundred feet down the throat of Asamayama, the great volcano. If the old lady had been impolite enough to stick out her tongue, I would at present be a cinder.

We started at seven in the evening on horseback. Now as you know I have ridden pretty much everything from a broom stick to a camel, but for absolute novelty of motion commend me to a Japanese horse. There is a lurch to larboard, then a lurch to starboard, with a sort of "shiver-my-timbers" interlude. A coolie walks at the head of each horse, and reasons softly with him when he misbehaves. We rode for thirteen miles to the foot of the volcano, then at one o'clock we left the horses with one of the men and began to climb. Each climber was tied to a coolie whose duty it was to pull, and to carry the lantern. We made a weird procession, and the strange call of the coolies as they bent their bodies to the task mingled with the laughter and exclamations of the party.

For some miles the pine trees and undergrowth covered the mountain, then came a stretch of utter barren-ness and isolation. Miles above yet seemingly close enough to touch rose tongues of flame and crimson smoke. Above was the majestic serenity of the summer night, below the peaceful valley, with the twinkling lights of far away villages. It was a queer sensation to be hanging thus between earth and sky, and to feel that the only thing between me and death was a small Japanese coolie, who was half dragging me up a mountain side that was so straight it was sway-back!

When at last we reached the top, daylight was showing

faintly in the east. Slowly and with a glory unspeakable the sun rose. The great flames and crimson smoke, which at night had appeared so dazzling, sank into insignificance. If anyone has the temerity to doubt the existence of a gracious, mighty God, let him stand at sunrise on the top of Asamayama and behold the wonder of His works!

I hardly dared to breathe for fear I would dispel the illusion, but a hearty lunch eaten with the edge of the crater for a table made things seem pretty real. The coming down was fearful for the ashes were very deep, and we often went in up to our knees.

The next morning at eleven, I rolled into my bed more dead than alive. My face and hands were blistered from the heat and the ashes, and I was sore from head to foot, but I had a vision in my soul that can never be effaced.

Hiroshima, September, 1904.

Well here I am back in H. (I used to think it stood for that too but it doesn't!) Curiously enough I rather enjoy getting back into harness this year. Three kindergartens to attend in the morning, class work in the afternoon, four separate accounts to be kept, besides housekeeping, mothers' meetings, and prayer meetings, would have appalled me once.

The only thing that phases me is the company. If only some nice accommodating cyclone would come along and gather up all the floating population, and deposit it in a neat pile in some distant fence corner, I would be everlastingly grateful. One loving brother wrote last week that he was coming with a wife and three children to board with us until his house was completed, and that he knew I would be glad to have them. Delighted I am sure! All I need to complete my checkered career is to keep a boarding-house! I smacked Susie Damn clear down the steps and sang "A consecrated cross-eyed bear," then I wrote him to come. It is against the principles of the school to refuse anyone its hospitality, consequently everybody who is out of a job comes to see us.

The waves of my wrath break upon Miss Lessing for allowing herself to be imposed upon, but she is as calm and serene as the Great Buddha of Kamakura.

My special grievance this morning is cooked tomatoes and baby organs. Our cook has just discovered cooked tomatoes, and they seem to fill some longfelt want in his soul. In spite of protest, he serves them to us for breakfast, tiffin and dinner, and the household sits with injured countenance, and silently holds me responsible. As for the nine and one wind bags that begin their wheezing and squeaking before breakfast, my thoughts are unfit for publication! This morning I was awakened by the strains "Shall we meet beyond the River?" Well if we do, the keys will fly that's all there is about it! Once in a while they side-track it to "Oh! to be nothing, nothing!" That is where I fully agree and if they would only give me a chance I would grant their desire in less time than it takes to write it. I am sure my Hades will be a hard seat in a lonesome corner where I must listen to baby organs all day and live on a perpetual diet of cooked tomatoes.

To-day they are bringing in the wounded soldiers from Liaoyang, and I try to keep away from the windows so I will not see them. Those bright strong boys that left here such a little while ago, are coming back on stretchers, crippled and disfigured for life.

Yesterday while taking a walk, I saw about two hundred men, right off the transport, waiting for the doctors and nurses to come. Men whose clothes had not been changed for weeks, ragged, bloody and soiled beyond conception. Wounded, tired, sick, with almost every trace of the human gone out of their faces, they sat or lay on the ground waiting to be cared for. Most of the wounds had not been touched since they were hastily tied up on the battlefield. I thought I had some idea of what war meant, but I hadn't the faintest conception of the real horror of it.

Miss Lessing is trying to get permission for us to do regular visiting at the hospitals, but the officials are very cautious about allowing any foreigner behind the scenes.

Just here I hung my head out of the window to ask the cook what time it was. He called back, "Me no know! clock him gone to sleep. He no talk some more."

I think I shall follow the example of the clock.

Hiroshima, October, 1904.

Dearest Mate:

I have been to the hospital at last and I can think of nothing, see nothing, and talk of nothing but those poor battered up men. Yesterday the authorities sent word that if the foreign teachers would come and make a little music for the sick men it would be appreciated. We had no musical instrument except the organ, so Miss Lessing and I bundled one up on a jinricksha and trudged along beside it through the street. I got almost hysterical over our absurd appearance, and pretended that Miss Lessing was the organ grinder, and I the monkey. But oh! Mate, when we got to the hospital all the silliness was knocked out of me. Thousands of mutilated and dying men, literally shot to pieces by the Russian bullets. I can't talk about it! It was too horrible to describe.

We wheeled the organ into one of the wards and two of the teachers sang while I played. It was pitiful to see how eager the men were to hear. The room was so big that those in the back begged to be moved closer, so the little nurses carried the convalescent ones forward on their backs.

For one hour I pumped away on that wheezy little old instrument, with the tears running down my cheeks most of the time. So long as I live I'll never make fun of a baby organ again. The joy that one gave that afternoon justified its being.

THE LADY OF THE DECORATION

And then—prepare for the worst,—we distributed tracts. Oh! yes I did it too, in spite of all the fun I have made, and would you believe it? those men who were able to walk, crowded around and *begged* for them, and the others in the beds held out their hands or followed us wistfully with their eyes. They were so crazy for something to read that they were even willing to read about the foreign God.

It was late when we got back and I went straight to bed and indulged in a chill. All the horror of war had come home to me for the first time, and my very soul rebelled against it. They say you get hardened to the sights after a few visits to the hospital, but I hope I shall never get to the point of believing that it's right for strong useful men to be killed or crippled for life in order to settle a controversy.

Before we went into the wards the physician in charge took us all over the buildings, showed us where the old bandages were being washed and cleaned, where the instruments were sharpened and repaired, where the stretchers and crutches, and "first aid to the injured" satchels were kept. We were taken through the post-office, where all the mail comes and goes from the front. It was touching to see the number of letters that had been sent home unopened.

Twenty thousand sick soldiers are cared for in Hiroshima, and such system, such cleanliness and order you have never seen. I have wished for Jack a thousand times; it would delight his soul to see the skill and ability of these wonderful little doctors and nurses.

Hiroshima, November, 1904.

To-morrow it will be four weeks since I have had any kind of mail from America. It seems to me that everything has stopped running across the ocean, even the waves.

I know little these days outside of the kindergarten and the hospital. The former grows cuter and dearer all the time. It is a constant inspiration to see the daily development of these cunning babies. As for the visits to the hospital, they are a self-appointed task that grows no easier through repetition. You know how I shrink from seeing pain, and how all my life I have tried to get away from the disagreeable? Well it is like torture to go day after day into the midst of the most terrible suffering. But in view of the bigger things of life, the tremendous struggle going on so near, the agony of the sick and wounded, the suffering of the women and children, my own little qualms get lost in the shuffle, and my one consuming desire is to help in any way I can.

Last week we took in addition to the "wind bag" two big baskets of flowers to give to the sickest ones. Oh! If I could only make you know what flowers mean to them! Men too sick to raise their heads and often dying, will stretch out their hands for a flower, and be perfectly content to hold it in their fingers. One soldier with both arms gone asked me for a flower just as I had emptied my basket. I would have given my month's salary for one rose, but all I had was a withered little pansy. He motioned for me to give him that and asked me to put it in a broken bottle hanging on the wall, so he could see it.

If I didn't get away from it all once in a while, I don't believe I could stand it. Yesterday was the Emperor's birthday and we had a holiday. I took several of the girls and went for a long ramble in the country. The fields were a brilliant yellow, rich and heavy with the unharvested grain. The mountains were deeply purple, and the sky so tenderly blue, that the whole world just seemed a place to be glad and happy in. Fall in Japan does not suggest death and decay, but rather the drifting into a beautiful rest, where dreams can be dreamed and the world forgot. Such a spirit of peace enveloped the whole scene, that it was hard to realize that the long line of black objects on the distant road were stretchers bearing the sick and wounded from the transports to the hospitals.

Hiroshima, December, 1904.

Last Saturday I had to go across the bay to visit one of our branch kindergartens. Many Russian prisoners are stationed on the island and I was tremendously interested in the good time they were having. The Japanese officials are entertaining them violently with concerts, picnics, etc. Imagine a lot of these big muscular men being sent on an all-day excursion with two little Japanese guards. Of course, it is practically impossible for the men to escape from the island but I don't believe they want to. A cook has actually been brought from Vladivostock so that they may have Russian food, and the best things in the markets are sent to them. The prisoners I saw seemed in high spirits, and were having as much fun as a lot of school boys out on a lark. I don't wonder! It is lots more comfortable being a prisoner in Japan than a soldier in Manchuria.

I only had a few minutes to visit the hospital, but I was glad I went. As the doctor took me through one of the wards where the sickest men lay, I saw one big rough looking Russian with such a scowl on his face that I hardly dared offer him my small posy. But I hated to pass him by so I ventured to lay it on the foot of the cot. What was my consternation when, after one glance, he clasped both hands over his face and sobbed like a sick child. "Are you in pain?" asked the doctor. "No," he said shortly, "I'm homesick." Oh! Mate, that finished me! Didn't I know better than anybody in the world how he felt? I just sat down on the side of the cot and patted him, and tried to tell him how sorry I was though he could hardly understand a word.

This morning I could have done a song and dance when I heard that he had been operated on and was to be sent home.

Almost every day we are having grand military funerals, and they are most impressive I can tell you. Yesterday twenty-two officers were buried at the same time, and the school stood on the street for over an hour to do them honor. The procession was very interesting, with the Buddhist priests, in their gorgeous robes, and the mourners in white or light blue. First came the square box with the cremated remains, then the officer's horse, then coolies carrying small trees which were to be planted on the grave. Next came a large picture of the deceased, and perhaps his coat or sword, next the shaven priests in magnificent raiment and last the mourners carrying small trays with rice cakes, to be placed upon the grave. The wives and mothers and daughters rode in jinrickshas, hand folded meekly in hand, and eyes downcast. Such calm resigned faces I have never seen, many white and wasted with sorrow, but under absolute control. Of the entire number only one gave vent to her grief; a bent old woman with thin grey hair cut close to her head, rode with both hands over her face. She had lost two sons in one battle, and the cry of her human heart was stronger than any precept of her religion.

HIROSHIMA, December, 1904.

You remember the Irishman's saying that we could be pretty comfortable in life if it wasn't for our pleasures? Well I could get along rather well in Japan were it not for the Merry Christmases. Such a terrible longing seizes me for my loved ones and for God's country that I feel like a needle near a magnet. But next Christmas! I just go right up in the air when I think about it.

This school of life is a difficult one at best, but when a weak sister like myself is put about three grades higher than she belongs, it is more than hard. I don't care a rap for the struggle and the heart aches, if I have only made good. When I came out there were two kindergartens, now there are nine besides a big training class. Anybody else could have done as much for the work but one thing is certain, the work couldn't have done for anyone else what it has done for me. Outwardly I am the same feather-weight as of old, but there is a big change inside, Mate, you'll have to take my word for it. I am coming to take the slaps of Fate very much as I used to take the curling of my hair with a hot iron, it pulled and sometimes burned, but I didn't care so long as it was going to improve my looks. So now I use my crosses as sort of curling irons for my character.

Your sudden decision to give up your trip to Europe this spring set me guessing! I can't imagine, after all your planning and your dreams, what could have changed your mind so completely. You don't seem to care a rap about going. Now look here, Mate, I want a full report. You have turned all the pockets of my confidence inside out. What about yours? Have you been getting an "aim" in life, are you going to be an operatic singer, or a temperance lecturer, or anything like that? You are so horribly high minded that I am prepared for the worst.

I wish it would stop raining. The mountains are hid by a heavy gray mist, and the drip, drip of the rain from roof

THE LADY OF THE DECORATION

and trees is not a cheering sound. I am doing my best to keep things bright within, I have built a big fire in my grate, and in my heart I have lighted all the lamps at my little shrines, and I am burning incense to the loves that were and are.

Just after tiffin the rain stopped for a little while and I rushed out for a walk. I had been reading the "Christmas Carol" all morning, and it brought so many memories of home that I was feeling rather wobbly. My walk set me up immensely. A baldheaded, toothless old man stopped me and asked me where I was "coming." When I told him he said that was wonderful and he hoped I would have a good time. A woman with a child on her back ran out and stopped me to ask if I would please let the baby see my hair. Half a dozen children and two dogs followed me all the way, and an old man and woman leaned against a wall and laughed aloud because a foreigner was so funny to look at.

If anyone thinks that he can indulge in a nice private case of the blues while taking a walk in Japan, he deceives himself. I started out feeling like Napoleon at St. Helena, and I came home cheerful and ravenously hungry.

I have been trying to read poetry this winter, but I don't make much progress. The truth is I have gained five pounds, and I am afraid I am getting too fat. I never knew but one fat person to appreciate poetry and he crocheted tidies.

By the way I have learned to knit!! You see there are so

many times when I have to play the gracious hostess when I feel like a volcano within, that I decided to get something on which I could vent my restlessness. It is astonishing how much bad temper one can knit into a garment. I don't know yet what mine is going to be, probably an opera bonnet for Susie Damn.

Kyoto, December, 1904.

You are not any more surprised to hear from me in Kyoto than I am to be here. One of the teachers here, a great big-hearted splendid woman, knowing that I was interested in the sick soldiers, asked me to come up for a week and help the Red Cross nurses. For six days we have met all the trains, and given hot tea, and books to both the men who were going to the front and to those who were being brought home. We work side by side with Buddhist priests, ladies of rank, and coolies, serving from one to four hundred men in fifteen minutes! You never saw such a scrimmage, everybody works like mad while the train stops, and the wild "Banzais" that greet us as the men catch sight of the hot tea, show us how welcome it is.

But the sights, Mate dear, are enough to break one's heart. I have seen good-byes, and partings until I haven't an emotion left! One man I talked with was going back for the fourth time having been wounded and sent home again and again; his wife never took her eyes from his face until the train pulled out, and the smile with which she sent him away was more heart rending than any tears I ever saw.

Then I have been touched by an old man and his wife who for four days have met every train to tell their only son good-bye. They are so feeble that they have to be helped up and down the steps and as each train comes and goes and their boy is not on board, they totter hand in hand back to the street corner to wait more long hours.

Going one way the trains carry the soldiers to the front, boys for the most part wild with enthusiasm, high spirits, and courage, and coming the other way in vastly greater numbers are the silent trains bearing the sick and wounded and dead.

We meet five trains during the day and one at two in the night. I have gotten so that I can sleep sitting upright on a hard bench between trains. Think of the plucky little Japanese women who have done this ever since the beginning of the war!

Out of my experience at the station came another very charming one yesterday. It seems that the president of the Red Cross Society is a royal princess, first cousin indeed to the Emperor. She had heard of me through her secretary and of the small services I had rendered here and at Hiroshima, so she requested an interview that she might thank me in person.

It seemed very ridiculous that I should receive formal recognition for pouring tea and handing out posies, but I was crazy to see the Princess, so early yesterday morning,

I donned my best raiment and sallied forth with an interpreter.

The house was a regular Chinese puzzle and I was passed on from one person to another until I got positively dizzy. At last we came to a long beautiful room, at the end of which, in a robe of purple and gold, all covered with white chrysanthemums, sat the royal lady. I was preparing to make my lowest bow, when, to my astonishment, she came forward with extended hand and spoke to me in English! Then she bowled me right over in the first round by asking me about Kindergarten. I forgot that she was a lady of royalty and numerous decorations, and that etiquette forbade me speaking except when spoken to. She was so responsive and so interested, that I found myself talking in a blue streak. Then she told me a bit of her story, and I longed to hear more. It seems that certain women of the royal line are not permitted to marry, and she, being restless and ambitious, became a Buddhist Priestess, having her own temple, priestesses, etc. The priestesses are all young girls, and I wish you could have seen them examining my clothes, my hair and my rings. The Princess herself is a woman of brilliant attainments, and fine executive ability.

Of course we had tea, and sat on the floor and chattered and laughed like a lot of school girls. When I left I was told that the Princess desired my photograph at once, and that I should sit for it the next day. I suppose I am in for it.

THE LADY OF THE DECORATION

Hiroshima, December, 1904.

My dearest Mate:

The American mail is in and the secret is out, or at least half-way out and I am wild with curiosity and interest. You say you can't give me any of the particulars and you would rather I wouldn't even guess. All that you want me to know is that you have "a new interest in life that is the deepest and most beautiful experience you have ever known." I will do as you request, not ask any questions, or make any surmises but you will let me say this, that no fame, no glory, no wealth can ever give one thousandth part of the real heart's content that one hour of love can give. Without it work of any kind is against the full tide, and accomplishment is emptier than vanity. The heart still cries out for its own, for what is its birthright and heritage.

I am glad with all my soul for your happiness, Mate, the tenderest blessing that lips could frame would not express half that is in my heart. There is nothing so sure in life as that love is best of all. You think you know it after a few weeks of loving, I know I know after years of grief and suffering and despair.

From the time when you used to stand between me and childish punishments, through all the happy days of girlhood, the sorrowful days of womanhood, on up to the bitter-sweet present, you have never failed me.

I want to give you a whole heart full of gladness and

rejoicing, I want to crowd out my own little wail of bereavement, but Oh! Mate, I never felt so alone in my life before! I am not asking you to tell me who the man is. I am trying not to *guess*. Tell me what you like and when you like, and rest assured that whatever comes, my heart is with you—and with him.

Hiroshima, January, 1905.

It has been longer than usual since I wrote but somehow things have been going wrong with me of late and I didn't want to bother you. But oh! Mate, I haven't anybody else in the world to come to, and you'll have to forgive me for bringing a cloud across your happiness.

The whole truth is I'm worsted! The fight has been too much. Days, weeks, months of homesickness have piled up on top of me until all my courage and my control, all my *will* seem paralysed.

Night after night I lie awake and stare out into the dark, and staring back at me is the one word "*alone*." In the daytime, I try to keep somebody with me all the time, I have gotten afraid of myself. My face in the mirror does not seem to belong to me, it is a curious unfamiliar face that I do not know. Every once in a while I want to beat the air and scream, but I don't do it. I clench my fists and set my teeth and teach, teach, teach.

But I can't go on like this forever! Flesh and spirit rebel

against a lifetime of it! Haven't I paid my penalty? Aren't the lightness and brightness and beauty ever coming back?

On my desk is a contract waiting to be signed for another four years at the school. Beside it is a letter from Brother, begging me to drop everything and come home at once. Can yon guess what the temptation is? On the one hand ceaseless work, uncongenial surroundings and exile, on the other luxury, loved ones,—and dependence. I must give my answer to-morrow and Heaven only knows what it will be. One thing is certain I am tired of doing hard things, I am tired of being brave.

It is storming fearfully but I am going out to mail this letter. If I cable that I am coming you must be the first one to know why. I have tried to grow into something higher and better, God knows I have, but I am afraid I am a house built on the sands after all. Don't be hard on me, Mate, whatever comes remember I have tried.

HIROSHIMA, 3 hours later.

If you open this letter first, don't read the one that comes in the same mail. I wrote it this afternoon, and I would give everything I possess to get it back again. When I went out to mail it, I was feeling so utterly desperate that I didn't care a rap for the storm or anything else. I went on and on until I came to the sea-wall that makes a big curve out into the sea. When I had gone as far as I dared, I climbed up on an old stone lantern, and let the spray and the rain beat on my face. The wind was whipping the waves into a perfect fury, and pounding them against the wall at my feet. The thunder rolled and roared, and great flashes of lightning ripped gashes in the green and purple water. It was the most glorious sight I ever saw! I felt that the wind, the waves, and the storm were all my friends and that they were doing all my beating and screaming for me.

I clung to the lantern, with my clothes dripping and my hair streaming about my face until the storm was over. And I don't think I was ever so near to God in my life as when the sun came out suddenly from the clouds and lit up that tempest-tossed sea into a perfect glory of light and color! And the peace had come into my heart, Mate, and I knew that I was going to take up my cross again and bear it bravely. I was so glad, so thankful that I could scarcely keep my feet on the ground. I struck out at full speed along the sea-wall and ran every step of the way home.

And now after a hot bath and dry clothes, with my little kettle singing by my side, I want to tell you that I have decided to stay, perhaps for five months, perhaps for five years.

Out of the wreckage of my old life I've managed to build a fairly respectable craft. It has taken me just four years to realize that it is not a pleasure boat. To-night I realize once for all that it is a very modest little tug, and wherever it can tow anything or anybody into harbor there it belongs, and there it stays.

Tell them all that I am quite well again, Mate, and as for you, please don't even bother your blessed head about me again. I have meekly taken my place in the middle of the sea-saw and I shall probably never go very high or very low again. I am sleepy for the first time in two weeks, so good-bye comrade mine and God bless you.

Hiroshima, February, 1905.

My dearest Mate:

I can't feel quite right until I tell you that I have guessed your secret, that I have known from the first it was Jack. I always knew you were made for each other, both so splendid and noble and true. It isn't any particular credit to you two that you are good, there was no alternative—you couldn't be bad.

How perfectly you will fit into all his plans and ambitions! A beautiful new life is opening up for you, a life so full of promise, of tremendous possibilities for good not only for you but for others that it seems like a bit of heaven.

Tell him how I feel, Mate. It is hard for me to write letters these days, but I want him to know that I am glad because he is happy.

I have been living in the past to-day going over the old days in the Mountains up at the lake, and the reunions on the farm. How many have gone down into the great silence since then! Somehow I seem nearer to them than

I do to you who are alive. While I am still on the crowded highway of life, yet I am surrounded by strange, unloving faces that have no connection with the joys or the sorrows of the past.

How the view changes as we pass along the great road. At first only the hilltops are visible, rosy and radiant under the enthusiasm of youth, then the level plains come into sight flooded with the bright light of mid-day, then slowly we slip into the valleys where the long shadows fall like memories across our hearts.

Oh! well, with all the struggles, all the heartaches, I am glad, Mate, very glad that I have lived—and laughed. For I am laughing again, in spite of the fact that my courage got fuddled and took the wrong road.

I heard of a man the other day who had received a sentence of fifteen years for some criminal act. He was in love with the freedom of life, he was young and strong, so he made a dash down a long iron staircase, dropped into a river, swam a mile and gained his freedom. All search failed to find him, but two days later he walked into the police station and gave himself up to serve his time. I made my dash for liberty, but I have come back to serve my time.

I don't have to tell you, Mate, that I am ashamed of having shown the white feather. You will write me a beautiful letter and explain it all away, but I know in my soul you are disappointed in me, and to even think about it is like going down in a swift elevator. Being able to go under gracefully is my highest ambition at present, but try as I will, I kick a few kicks before I disappear.

Please, please, Mate, don't worry about me. I promise that if I reach the real limit I will cable for a special steamer to be sent for me. But I don't intend to reach it, or at least I am going to get on the other side of it, so there will be no further danger.

Two long months will pass before I get an answer to this. It will come in April with the cherry blossoms and the spring.

Hiroshima, March, 1905.

You must forgive me if the letters have been few and far between lately. After my little "wobble" I plunged into work with might and main, and I am still at it for all I am worth. First I house-cleaned, and the old place must certainly be surprised at its transformation. Fresh curtains, new paper, cozy window seats, and bright cushions have made a vast difference. Then I tackled the kindergarten, and the result is about the prettiest thing in Japan. The room is painted white with buff walls and soft muslin curtains, the only decoration being a hundred blessed babies, in gay little kimonas, who look like big bunches of flowers placed in a wreath upon the floor.

As for my training class, I have no words to express my gratification. I can scarcely believe that the fine, capable, earnest young women that are going out to all parts of

Japan to start new Kindergartens, are the timid, giggling, dependent little creatures that came to me four years ago.

Goodness knows I was as immature in my way as they were in theirs, but in my desperate need, I builded better than I knew. I recklessly followed your advice and hitched my little go-cart to a star, and the star turned into a meteor and is now whizzing through space getting bigger and stronger all the time, and I am tied on to the end of it unable to stop it or myself.

If I only had more sense and more ability, think what I might have done!

The work at the hospital is still very heavy. The wards are bare and repellant and the days are long and dreary for the sick men. We do all we can to cheer them up, have phonograph concerts, magic lantern shows, with the magic missing, and baby organ recitals. The results are often ludicrous, but the appreciation of the men for our slightest effort is so hearty that it more than repays us.

I saw one man yesterday who had gone crazy on the battlefield. He looked like a terror stricken animal afraid of everybody, and hiding under the sheet at the slightest approach. When I came in he cowered back against the wall shaking from head to foot. I put a big bunch of flowers on the bed, and in a flash his hands were stretched out for them, and a smile came to his lips. After that whenever I passed the door, he would shout out, "Arigato! Arigato!" which the nurse said was the first sign of sanity he had shown.

THE LADY OF THE DECORATION

In the next room was a man who had fallen from a mast on one of the flag ships. He had landed full on his face and the result was too fearful to describe. The nurse said he could not live through the night so I laid my flowers on his bed and was slipping out when he called to me. His whole head was covered with bandages except his mouth and one eye, and I had to lean down very close to understand what he said. What do you suppose he wanted? To look at my hat!! He had never seen one before and he was just like a child in his curiosity.

Of course, as foreigners, we always excite comment, and are gazed at, examined and talked about continually. I sometimes feel like a wild animal in a cage straight from the heart of Africa!

Our unfailing point of contact is the flowers. You cannot imagine how they love them. I have seen men holding them tenderly in their fingers and talking to them as they would to children. Imagine retreating soldiers after a hard day's fight, stopping to put a flower in a dead comrade's hand!

Oh! Mate, the most comical things and the most tragic, the most horrible and the most beautiful are all mixed up together. Every time I go to the hospital I am faced with my wasted years of opportunities. It takes so little to bring sunshine and cheer, and yet millions of us go chasing our own little desires through life, and never stop to think of the ones who are down.

No, I am not going to turn Missionary nor Salvation

Army lassie, but with God's help I shall serve somewhere and "good cheer for the lonely" shall be my watch-word.

I am lots better than I was, though I am still tussling with insomnia. My crazy nerves play me all sorts of tricks, but praise be I have stopped worrying. I have come at last to see that God has found even a small broken instrument like myself worth working through, and I just lift up my heart to Him every day, battered and bruised as it is, in deep unspeakable thankfulness.

Hiroshima, April, 1905.

My dearest Mate:

Your letter is here and I haven't a grain of sense, nor dignity, nor anything else except a wild desire to hug everything in sight! I am having as many thrills as a surcharged electric battery, and I am so hysterically happy that I don't care what I do or say.

Why didn't you tell me at first it was Dr. Leet? My mind was so full of Jack that I forgot that other men inhabited the earth. It is no use bluffing any longer, Mate, there has never been a minute since the train pulled out of the home station that every instinct in me hasn't cried out for Jack. Pride kept me silent at first, and then the miserable thought got hold of me that he was beginning to care for you. Oh! the agony I have suffered, trying to be loyal to you, to be generous to him, and to put myself out of the question! And now your blessed letter comes, and laughs at my fears and says "Jack chooses his wife as he does his friends, for eternity."

I have no words to fit the occasion, all I can say is now that happiness has shown me the back of her head I am scared to death to look her in the face. But I "shore do" like the arrangement of her back hair.

Don't breathe a word of what I have written, but as you love me find out absolutely and beyond all possibility of doubt if Jack feels exactly as he did four years ago. If you give me your word of honor that he does, then—I will write.

I have signed a contract for another year, and I must stay it out, but I would spend a year in Hades if Heaven was at the end of it.

All you say about Dr. Leet fills me with joy. He does not need any higher commendation in this world nor the next than that you are willing to marry him! Isn't it dandy that he is going to back the hospital scheme? When I think of the way Jack has worked for ten years without a vacation, putting all his magnificent ability, his strength, his youth, his health even into that project, I don't wonder that men like Dr. Leet are eager to put their money and services at his disposal. You say Dr. Leet does it upon the condition that Jack takes a rest. Make him stick to it, Mate, he will kill himself if he isn't stopped.

I have read your letters over and over and traced your love affair every inch of the way. Why are you such an old clam! To think that I am the only one that knows your secret, and that up to to-day I have been barking up the wrong tree! Never mind, I forgive you, I forgive everybody, I am drunk with happiness and generous in consequence.

My little old lane is glorified, even the barbed wire fence on either side scintillates. The house is too small, I am going out on the River Road, and see the cherry blossoms on the hill sides and the sunlight on the water, and feel the road under my feet. I feel like a prospector who has struck gold. Whatever comes of it all, for this one day I am going to give full rein to my fancy and be gloriously happy once more.

Hiroshima, May, 1905.

There is a big yellow bee, doing the buzzing act in the sunshine on my window, and I am just wondering who is doing the most buzzing, he or I? His nose is yellow with pollen from some flower he has robbed, his body is fat and lazy, all in all he is about the happiest bee I ever beheld. But I can go him one better, while it is only his wings that are beating with happiness, it is my heart that is going to the tune of rag-time jigs and triumphal alleluias all at the same time.

My chef, four feet two, remarked this morning "Sensei happy all same like chicken!" He meant bird, but any old fowl will do.

THE LADY OF THE DECORATION

Oh! Mate, it is good to be alive these days. For weeks we have had nothing but glorious sunrises, gorgeous sunsets, and perfect noondays. The wistaria has come before the cherry blossoms have quite gone, and the earth is a glow of purple and pink with the blue sky above as tender as love.

Each morning I open my windows to the east to see the marvel of a new day coming fresh from the hands of its Maker, and each evening I stand at the opposite window and watch the same day drop over the mountains to eternity. In the flaming sky where so often hangs the silver crescent is always the promise of another day, another chance to begin anew.

Just one more year and I will be turning the gladdest face homeward that ever a lonely pilgrim faced the West with. There will be many a pang at leaving Japan, I have learned life's deepest lesson here, and the loneliness and isolation that have been so hard to bear have revealed inner depths of which I never dreamed before. What strange things human beings are! Our very crosses get dear after we have carried them awhile!

I have had three offers to sign fresh contracts, Nagasaki, Tokyo, and here, but I am leaving things to shape themselves for the future. Whatever happens I am coming home first. If happiness is waiting for me, I'll meet it with outstretched arms, if not I am coming back to my post. Thank God I am sure of myself at last!

The work at the hospital this month is much lighter, and the patients are leaving for home daily. The talk of peace is in the air, and we are praying with all our hearts that it may come. Nobody but those who have seen with their own eyes can know the unspeakable horrors of this war. It is not only those who are fighting at the front who have known the full tragedy, it is those also who are fighting at home the relentless foe of poverty, sickness, and desolation. If victory comes to Japan, half the glory must be for those silent heroic little women, who gave their all, then took up the man's burden and cheerfully bore it to the end.

I was very much interested in your account of the young missionary who is coming through Japan on her way to China. I know just how she will feel when she steps off the steamer and finds no friendly face to welcome her. I talked over your little scheme with Miss Lessing and she says I can go up to Yokohama in July to meet her and bring her right down here. Tell her to tie her handkerchief around her arm so I will know her, and not to worry the least bit, that I will take care of her and treat her like one of my own family.

Can you guess how eagerly I am waiting for your answer to my April letter? It cannot come before the last of June, and happy as I am, the time seems very long. Yet I would rather live to the last of my days like this, travelling ever toward the pot of gold at the end of the rainbow, than ever to arrive and find the gold not there!

You say that at last you know I am the "captain of my soul." Well, Mate, I believe I am, but I just want to say that it's a hard worked captain that I am, and if anybody wants

THE LADY OF THE DECORATION

the job—very much—I think he can get it.

Yokohama, July 5, 1905.

Do you suppose, if people could, they would write letters as soon as they got to Heaven! I don't know where to begin nor what to say. The only thing about me that is on earth is this pen point, the rest is floating around in a diamond-studded, rose-colored mist!

I will try to be sensible and give you some idea of what has been happening, but how I am to get it on paper I don't know. I got here yesterday, the 4th of July, on the early train, and rushed down to the hatoba to meet the launch when it came in from the steamer. I had had no breakfast and was as nervous as a witch. Your letter had not come, and my fears were increasing every moment.

Well I took my place on the steps as the launch landed and waited, with very little interest I must confess, for your young missionary to appear. By and by I saw a handkerchief tied to a sleeve, but it was a man's sleeve. I gave one more look, and my heart seemed to stop. "Jack!" I cried, and then everything went black before me, and I didn't know anything more. It was the first time I ever fainted; sorrow and grief never knocked me out, but joy like that was enough to kill me!

When I came to, I was at the hotel and I didn't dare open my eyes—I knew it was all a dream, and I did not want to come back to reality. I lay there holding on to the vision, until I heard a man's voice close by say, "She will be all right now, I will take care of her." Then I opened my eyes, and with three Japanese maids and four Japanese men and two ladies off the steamer looking on, I flung my arms about Jack's neck and cried down his collar!

He made me stay quiet all morning, and just before tiffin he calmly informed me that he had made all the arrangements for us to be married at three o'clock. I declared I couldn't, that I had signed a contract for another year at Hiroshima, that Miss Lessing would think I was crazy, that I must make some plans. But you know Jack! He met every objection that I could offer, said he would see Miss Lessing and make it all right about the contract, that I was too nervous to teach any more, and last that I owed him a little consideration after four years of waiting. Then I realized how the lines had deepened in his face, and how the grey was streaking his hair, and I surrendered promptly.

We were married in a little English church on the Bluff, with half a dozen witnesses. Several Americans whom Jack had met on the steamer, a missionary friend of mine, and the Japanese clerk constituted the audience.

It is all like a beautiful dream to me still, and I am afraid to let Jack get out of my sight for fear I will wake up. It was Fourth of July, and Christmas, and birthday, and wedding day all rolled into one. The whole city was celebrating, the hotel a flutter of flags and ribbons, the bay full of every kind of pleasure craft. At night there was a grand lantern fete and fireworks, and a huge figure of Uncle Sam with stars in his coat tails. Thousands of Japanese in their gayest kimonas thronged the Bund, listening to the music, watching the foreigners and the fire-works.

Jack and I were like two children, he forgot that he was a staid doctor, and I forgot that I had ever been a Foreign Missionary Kindergarten teacher. We were boy and girl again and up to our eyes in love. It was the first Fourth of July for fifteen years that I did not have some unhappiness to conceal. As one of my girls said about herself: "My little lonely heart had flewed away!"

All the loneliness, the heartaches, the pains are justified now. I do not regret the past for through it the present is.

Do you remember the lines: "He shall restore the years that the locust hath eaten?" Well I believe that while I have been struggling out here, He has restored them, and that I will be permitted to return to a new life, a life given back by God.

Of course you know we are going on around. It seems rather inconsistent to say I am glad of it after all my wailing for home. The truth is, home has come to *me*!

Jack says we are to meet you and Dr. Leet in Paris. You needn't try to persuade me that Heaven will be any better than the present!

There is no use in my trying to thank you for your part in all this, dear Mate. I have been in a chronic state of gratitude to you ever since I was born! I can only say with all my heart and soul "God bless you and Good-bye."

P.S. In my wedding ring is engraved M.L.O.T.D. Can you guess what it means?

THE LADY
AND SADA SAN

*To
Ellen Churchill Semple
and
Charlotte Smith
My Fellow Wanderers Through the Orient*

On the High Seas. June, 1911.

Mate:

You once told me, before you went to Italy, that after having been my intimate relative all these years, you had drawn a red line through the word surprise. Restore the abused thing to its own at once. You will need it when the end of this letter is reached. I have left Kentucky after nine years of stay-at-home happiness, and once again I am on my way to Japan—this time in wifely disobedience to Jack's wishes.

What do you think that same Jack has "gone and done"! Of course he is right. That is the provoking part of Jack; it always turns out that he is in the right. Two months ago he went to some place in China which, from its ungodly name, should be in the furthermost parts of a wilderness. Perhaps you have snatched enough time from guarding the kiddies from a premature end in Como to read a headline or so in the home papers. If by some wonderful chance, between baby prattle, bumps and measles, they have given you a moment's respite, then you know that the Government has grown decidedly restless for fear the energetic and enterprising bubonic or pneumonic germ might take passage on some of the ships from the Orient. So it is fortifying against invasion. The Government, knowing Jack's indomitable determination to learn everything knowable about the private life and character of a given germ, asked him to join several other men it is sending out to get information, provided of course the germ doesn't get them first.

Jack read me the official-looking document one night between puffs of his after-dinner pipe.

Another surprise awaits you. For once in my life I had nothing to say. Possibly it is just as well for the good of the cause that the honorable writer of the letter could not see how my thoughts looked.

I glanced about our little den, aglow with soft lights; everything in it seemed to smile. Well, as you know it, Mate, I do not believe even you realize the blissfulness of the hours of quiet comradeship we have spent there. With the great know-it-all old world shut out, for joyful years we have dwelt together in a home-made paradise. And yet it seemed just then as if I were dwelling in a home-made Other Place.

The difference in the speed of time depends on whether love is your guest or not.

The thought of the briefest interruption to my content made me feel like cold storage. A break in happiness is sometimes hard to mend. The blossom does not return to the tree after the storm, no matter how beautiful the sunshine; and the awful fear of the faintest echo of past sorrow made my heart as numb as a snowball. To the old terror of loneliness was added fear for Jack's safety. But I did not do what you naturally would prophesy. After seeing the look on Jack's face I changed my mind, and my protest was the silent kind that says so much. It was lost! Already Jack had gone into one of his trances, as he does whenever there is a possibility of bearding a brand-new microbe in its den, whether it is in his own country or one beyond the seas. In body he was in a padded chair with all the comforts of home and a charming wife within speaking distance. In spirit he was in dust-laden China, joyfully following the trail of the wandering germ. Later on, when Jack came to, we talked it over. I truly remembered your warnings on the danger of impetuosity; for I choked off every hasty word and gave my consent for Jack to go. Then I cried half the night because I had.

We both know that long ago Jack headed for the topmost rung of a very tall scientific ladder. Sometimes my enthusiasm as chief booster and encourager has failed, as when it meant absence and risk. Though I have known women who specialized in renunciation, till they were the only happy people in the neighborhood, its charms have never lured me into any violent sacrifice. Here was my chance and I firmly refused to be the millstone to ornament Jack's neck.

You might know, Mate? I was hoping all the time that he would find it quite impossible to leave such a nice biddable wife at home. But I learn something new about Jack every day. After rather heated discussion it was decided that I should stay in the little home. That is, the heat and the discussion was all on my side. The decision lay in the set of Jack's mouth, despite the tenderness in his eyes. He thought the risks of the journey too great for me; the hardships of the rough life too much. Dear me! Will men never learn that hardship and risk are double cousins to loneliness, and not even related to love by marriage?

But just as well paint on water as to argue with a scientist when he has reached a conclusion.

Besides, said Jack, the fatherly Government has no intention that petticoats, even hobbled ones, should be flitting around while the habits and the methods of the busy insect were being examined through a microscope or a telescope. The choice of instrument depending, of course, upon the activity of the bug.

Black Charity was to be my chief-of-police and comforter-in-general. Parties—house, card and otherwise—were to be my diversion, and I was to make any little trips I cared for. Well, that's just what I am doing. Of course, there might be a difference of opinion as to whether a journey from Kentucky to Japan is a *little* trip.

I am held by a vague uneasiness today. Possibly it's because I am not certain as to Jack's attitude, when he learns through my letter, which is sailing along with me, that I am going to Japan to be as near him as possible. I hope he will appreciate my thoughtfulness in saving him all the bother of saying no. Or it might be that my slightly dampened spirits come from the discussion I am still having with myself whether it's the part of a dutiful wife to present herself a wiggling sacrifice to science, or whether science should attend to its own business and lead not into temptation the scientifically inclined heads of peaceful households.

You'll say the decision of what was best lay with Jack. Honey, there's the error of your mortal mind! In a question like that my spouse is as one-sided as a Civil War veteran. Say germ-hunt to Jack and it's like dangling a gaudy fly before a hungry carp.

I saw Jack off at the station, and went back to the little house. Charity had sent the cook home and with her own hands served all the beloved dainties of my long-ago childhood, trying to coax me into forgetfulness. As you remember, Mate, dinner has always been the happiest hour of the day in our small domain. Now? Well, everything was just the same. The only difference was Jack. And the half circle of bare tablecloth opposite me was about as cheerful as a snowy afternoon at the North Pole. I wandered around the house for awhile, but every time I turned a corner there was a memory waiting to greet me. Now the merriest of them seemed to be covered with a chilly shadow, and every one was pale and ghostly. All night I lay awake, playing at the old game of mental solitaire and keeping tryst with the wind which seemed to tap with unseen fingers at my window and sigh,

> "Then let come what come may
> .   .   .   .   .
> I shall have had my day."

Is it possible, Mate, that my glorious day, which I thought

had barely tipped the hour of noon, is already lengthening into the still shadows of evening?

It was foolish but, for the small comfort I got out of it, I turned on the light and looked inside my wedding-ring. Time has worn it a bit but the letters which spell "My Lady of the Decoration," spelled again the old-time thrill into my heart.

What's the use of tying your heartstrings around a man, and then have ambition slip the knot and leave you all a-quiver?

Far be it from me to stand in Jack's way if germ-stalking is necessary to his success. Just the same, I could have spent profitable moments reading the burial service over every microbe, home-grown and foreign.

Really, Mate, I've conscientiously tried every plan Jack proposed and a few of my own. It was no use. That day-after-Christmas feeling promptly suppressed any effort towards contentment.

At first there was a certain exhilaration in catching pace with the gay whirl which for so long had been passed by for homier things. You will remember there was a time when the pace of that same whirl was never swift enough for me; but my taste for it now was gone, and it was like trying to do a two-step to a funeral march. For once in my life I knew the real meaning of that poor old worn-to-a-frazzle call of the East, for now the dominant note was the call of love.

I heard it above the clink of the teacups. It was in the

THE LADY AND SADA SAN

swish of every silk petticoat. If I went to the theater, church or concert, the call of that germ-ridden spot of the unholy name beat into my brain with the persistency of a tom-tom on a Chinese holiday.

Say what you will, Mate, it once took all my courage to leave those I loved best and go to far-away Japan. Now it required more than I could dig up to *stay*—with the best on the other side of the Pacific.

The struggle was easy and swift. The tom-tom won and I am on my way to be next-door neighbor to Jack.

Those whom it concerned here were away from home, so I told no one good-by, thus saving everybody so much wasted advice. If there were a tax on advice the necessities of life would not come so high. Charity followed me to the train, protesting to the last that "Marse Jack gwine doubt her velocity when she tell him de truf bout her lady going a-gaddin' off by herse'f and payin' no mind to her ole mammy's prosterations." I asked her to come with me as maid. She refused; said her church was to have an ice-cream sociable and she had "to fry de fish."

This letter will find you joyfully busy with the babies and the "only man." Blest woman that you are.

But I know you. I have a feeling that you have a few remarks to make. So hurry up. Let us get it off our minds. Then I can better tell you what I am doing. Something is going to happen. It usually does when I am around. I have been asked to chaperone a young girl whose face and name spell romance. If I were seeking occupation here is the opportunity knocking my door into splinters.

Still at Sea. June, 1911.

Any time you are out of a job and want to overwork all your faculties and a few emotions, try chaperoning a young room-mate answering to the name of Sada San, who is one-half American dash, and the other half the unnamable witchery of a Japanese woman; a girl with the notes of a lark in her voice when she sings to the soft twang of an old guitar.

If, too, you are seeking to study psychological effect of such a combination on people, good, middlin' and otherwise, I would suggest a Pacific liner as offering fifty-seven varieties, and then some.

The last twinge of conscience I had over coming, died a cheerful death. I'd do it again. For not only is romance surcharging the air, but fate gives promise of weaving an intricate pattern in the story of this maid whose life is just fairly begun and whom the luck of the road has given me as traveling mate. Now, remembering a few biffs fate has given me, I have no burning desire to meddle with her business. Neither am I hungering for responsibility. But what are you going to say to yourself, when a young girl with a look in her eyes you would wish your daughter to have, unhesitatingly gives you a letter addressed at large to some "Christian Sister"! You read it to find it's from

THE LADY AND SADA SAN

her home pastor, requesting just a little companionship for "a tender young soul who is trying her wings for the first time in the big and beautiful world"! I have a very private opinion about reading my title clear to the Christian Sister business, but no woman with a heart as big as a pinch of snuff could resist giving her very best and much more to the slip of a winsome maid, who confidingly asks it—especially if the sister has any knowledge of the shadows lurking in the beautiful world.

Mate, these steamers as they sail from shore to shore are like giant theaters. Every trip is an impromptu drama where comedy, farce, and often startling tragedy offer large speaking parts. The revelation of human nature in the original package is funny and pathetic. Amusement is always on tap and life stories are just hanging out of the port-hole waiting to attack your sympathy or tickle your funny bone. But you'd have to travel far to find the beginning of a story so heaped up with romantic interest as that of Sada San as she told it to me, one long, lazy afternoon as I lay on the couch in my cabin, thanking my stars I was getting the best of the bare tablecloth and the empty house at home.

Some twenty years ago Sada's father, an American, grew tired of the slow life in a slow town and lent ear to the fairy stories told of the Far East, where fortunes were made by looking wise for a few moments every morning and devoting the rest of the day to samisens and flutes. He found the glorious country of Japan. The beguiling tea-houses, and softly swinging sampans were all too distracting. They sang ambition to sleep and the fortune escaped.

He drifted, and at last sought a mean existence as teacher of English in a school of a remote seaside village. His spirit broke when the message came of the death of the girl in America who was waiting for him. Isolation from his kind and bitter hours left for thought made life alone too ghastly. He tried to make it more endurable by taking the pretty daughter of the head man of the village as his wife.

My temperature took a tumble when I saw proofs of a hard and fast marriage ceremony, signed and countersigned by a missionary brother who meant business.

You say it is a sordid tale? Mate, I know a certain spot in this Land of Blossoms, where only foreigners are laid to rest, which bears testimony to a hundred of its kind—strange and pitiful destinies begun with high and brilliant hopes in their native land; and when illusions have faded, the end has borne the stamp of tragedy, because suicide proved the open door out of a life of failure and exile.

Sada's father was saved suicide and long unhappiness by a timely tidal-wave, which swept the village nearly bare, and carried the man and his wife out to sea and to eternity.

The child was found by Susan West who came from a neighboring town to care for the sick and hungry. Susan was a teacher-missionary. Not much to look at, if her picture told the truth, but from bits of her history that I've picked up her life was a brighter jewel than most of us

THE LADY AND SADA SAN

will ever find in a heavenly crown. Instead of holding the unbeliever by the nape of the neck and thrusting a not-understood doctrine down his unwilling throat, she lived the simple creed of loving her neighbor better than herself. And the old pair of goggles she wore made little halos around the least speck of good she found in any transgressor, no matter how warped with evil.

When she wasn't helping some helpless sinner to see the rainbow of promise at the end of the straight and narrow way, Susan spent her time and all her salary, giving sick babies a fighting chance for life. She took the half-drowned little Sada home with her, and searched for any kinsman left the child. There was only one, her mother's brother. He was very poor and gladly gave his consent that Miss West should keep the child—as long as it was a girl! Susan had taught the man English once in the long ago and this was his chance to repay her.

Later on when the teacher found her health failing and headed for home in America, Uncle Mura was still more generous and raised no objections to her taking the baby with her.

Together they lived in a small Western town. The missionary reared the child by rule of love only and went on short rations to educate her. Sada's eager mind absorbed everything offered her like a young sponge, and when a few months ago Susanna folded her hands and joined her foremothers, there was let loose on the world this exquisite girl with her solitary legacy of untried ideals and a blind enthusiasm for her mother's people.

Right here, Mate, was when I had a prolonged attack of cold shivers. Just before Miss West passed along, knowing that the Valley was near, she wrote to Uncle in Japan and told him that his niece would soon be alone. Can't you imagine the picture she drew of her foster child who had satisfied every craving of her big mother heart? Fascinating and charming and so weighted with possibilities, that Mura, who had prospered, leaped for his chance and sent Sada San money for the passage over.

Not a mite of anxiety shadowed her eyes when she told me that Uncle kept a wonderful tea-house in Kioto. He must be very rich, she thought, because he wrote her of the beautiful things she was to have. About this time the room seemed suffocating. I got up and turned on the electric fan. The only thing required of her, she continued, was to use her voice to entertain Uncle's friends. But she hoped to do much more. Through Miss West she knew how many of her mother's dear people needed help. How glorious that she was young and strong and could give so much. Susan had also talked to her of the flowers, the lovely scenery, the poetry of the people and their splendid spirit—making a dreamland where even man was perfect. How she loved it! How proud she was to feel that in part it was her country. Faithfully would she serve it. Oh, Susanna West! I'd like to shake you till your harp snapped a string. It's like sending a baby to pick flowers on the edge of a bottomless pit.

What could I say! The missionary-teacher had told the

truth. She simply failed to mention that in the fairy-land there are cherry-blossom lanes down which no human can wander without being torn by the brier patches.

The path usually starts from a wonderful tea-house where Uncles have grown rich. Miss West didn't mean to shirk her duty. In most things the begoggled lady was a visionary with a theory that if you don't talk about a thing it does not exist; and like most of her kind she swept the disagreeables into a dust heap and made for the high places where all was lovely. And yet she had toiled with the girl through all the difficulties of the Japanese language; and, to give her a musical education, had pinched to the point of buying one hat in eight years!

Now it is all done and Sada is launched on the high seas of life with a pleasure-house for a home and an unscrupulous Uncle with unlimited authority for a chaperon. Shades of Susan! but I am hoping guardian angels are "really truly," even if invisible.

Good night, Mate. This game of playing tag with jarring thoughts, new and old, has made six extra wrinkles. I am glad I came and you and Jack will have to be, for to quote Charity, "I'se done resoluted on my word of honah" to keep my hands, if possible, on Sada whose eyes are as blue as her hair is black.

Pacific Ocean.

Since morning the sea has been a sheet of blue, streaked with the silver of flying fish. That is all the scenery there is; not a sail nor a bird nor an insect. Either the unchanging view or something in the air has stimulated everybody into being their nicest. It is surprising how quickly graciousness possesses some people when there is a witching girl around. Vivacious young men and benevolent officers have suddenly appeared out of nowhere, spick and span in white duck and their winningest smiles. Entertainments dovetail till there is barely time for change of costume between acts.

But let me tell you, Mate, living up to being a mother is no idle pastime, particularly if it means reviving the lost art of managing love-smitten youths and elderly male coquettes. There is a specimen of each opposite Sada and me at table who are so generous with their company on deck, before and after meals, I have almost run out of excuses and am short on plans to avoid the heavy obligations of their eager attentions.

The youth is a To-Be-Ruler of many people, a Maharajah of India. But the name is bigger than the man. Two years ago his father started the boy around the world with a sack full of rubles and a head full of ancient Indian lore. With these assets he paused at Oxford that he might skim through the classics. He had been told this was where all

THE LADY AND SADA SAN

the going-to-be-great men stopped to acquire just the proper tone of superiority so necessary in ruling a country. Of course he picked up a bit on electricity, mechanics, etc. This accomplished to his satisfaction he ran over to America to view the barbarians' god of money and take a glance at their houses which touched the sky. But his whole purpose in living, he told me, was to yield himself to certain meditations, so that in his final reincarnation, which was only a few centuries off, he would return to the real thing in Buddha. In the meantime he was to be a lion, a tiger and a little white bird. At present he is plain human, with the world-old malady gnawing at his heart, a pain which threatens to send his cogitations whooping down a thornier and rosier lane than any Buddha ever knew. Besides I am thinking a few worldly vanities have crept in and set him back an eon or so. He wears purple socks, pink ties and a dainty watch strapped around his childish wrist.

When I asked him what impressed him most in America, he promptly answered with his eyes on Sada, "Them girls. They are rapturous!"

Farewell Nirvana! With a camp stool in one hand and a rosary in the other, he follows Sada San like the shadow on a sun dial. Wherever she is seated, there is the stool and the royal youth, his mournful eyes feasting on the curves and dimples of her face, her lightest jest far sweeter than any prayer, the beads in his hand forgotten.

The other would-be swain calls himself a Seeker of Truth. Incidentally he is hunting a wife. His general attitude is a constant reminder of the uncertainty of life. His presence makes you glad that nothing lasts. He says his days are heavy with the problems of the universe, but you can see for yourself that this very commercial traveler carries a light side line in an assortment of flirtations that surely must be like dancing little sunbeams on a life of gloom.

Goodness knows how much of a nuisance he would be if it were not for a little lady named Dolly, who sits beside him, gray in color, dress and experience. At no uncertain age she has found a belated youthfulness and is starting on the first pleasure trip of her life.

Coming across the country to San Francisco, her train was wrecked. In the smash-up a rude chair struck her just south of the belt line and she fears brain fever from the blow. The alarm is not general, for though just freed by kind death from an unhappy life sentence of matrimony she is ready to try another jailer.

Whether he spied Dolly first and hoped that the gleam from her many jewels would light up the path in his search for Truth and a few other things, or whether the Seeker was sought, I do not know. However the flirtation which seems to have no age limit has flourished like a bamboo tree. For once the man was too earnest. Dolly gave heed and promptly attached herself with the persistency of a barnacle to a weather-beaten junk. By devices worthy a finished fisher of men, she holds him to his job of suitor, and if in a moment of abstraction his would-be ardor for Sada grows too perceptible, the little lady reels in a yard or so of line to make sure her prize is still dangling on the hook.

To-day at tiffin the griefless widow unconsciously scored at the expense of the Seeker, to the delight of the whole table. For Sada's benefit this man quoted a long passage from some German philosopher. At least it sounded like that. It was far above the little gray head he was trying to ignore and so weighty I feared for her mentality. But I did not know Dolly. She rose like a doughnut. Looking like a child who delights in the rhythm of meaningless sounds, she heard him through, then exclaimed with breathless delight, "Oh, ain't he fluid!"

The man fled, but not before he had asked Sada for two dances at night.

It is like a funny little curtain-raiser, with jealousy as a gray-haired Cupid. So far as Sada is concerned, it is admiration gone to waste. Even if she were not gaily indifferent, she is too absorbed in the happy days she thinks are awaiting her. Poor child! Little she knows of the limited possibilities of a Japanese girl's life; and what the effect of the painful restrictions will be on one of her rearing, I dare not think.

Once she is under the authority of Uncle, the Prince, the Seeker, and all mankind will be swept into oblivion; and, until such time as she can be married profitably and to her master's liking, she will know no man. The cruelest awakening she will face is the attitude of the Orient toward the innocent offspring in whose veins runs the blood of two races, separated by differences which never have been and never will be overcome.

In America the girl's way would not have been so hard because her novel charm would have carried her far. But *hear me:* in Japan, the very wave in her hair and the color of her eyes will prove a barrier to the highest and best in the land. Even with youth and beauty and intelligence, unqualified recognition for the Eurasian is as rare as a square egg.

Another thought hits me in the face as if suddenly meeting a cross bumblebee. Will the teachings of the woman, who lived with her head in the clouds, hold hard and fast when Uncle puts on the screws?

The Seeker says it is the fellow who thinks first that wins. He speaks feelingly on the subject. Right now I am going to begin cultivating first thought, and try to be near if danger, whose name is Uncle, threatens the girl who has walked into my affections and made herself at home.

Later.

All the very good people are in bed. The very worldly minded and the young are on deck reluctantly finishing the last dance under a canopy of make-believe cherry blossoms and wistaria. I am on the deck between, closing this letter to you which I will mail in Yokohama in a few hours.

In a way I shall be glad to see a quiet room in a hotel

and hie me back to simple living, free from the responsibilities of a temporary parent. I am not promising myself any gay thrills in the meantime. What's the use, with Jack on the borderland of a sulphurous country and you in the Garden of Eden? His letters and yours will be my greatest excitement. So write and keep on writing and never fear that I will not do the same. You are the safety-valve for my speaking emotions, Mate; so let that help you bear it.

Please mark with red ink one small detail of Sada's story. When I was fastening her simple white gown for the dance her chatter was like that of a sunny-hearted child. Indeed, she liked to dance. Susan did not think it harmful. She said if your heart was right your feet would follow. When Miss West could spare her she always went to parties with *Billy*, and oh, how he could dance if he was so big and had red hair.

So! there was a Billy? I looked in her face for signs. The way was clear but there was a soft little quiver in her voice that caused me carefully to label the unknown William, and lay him on a shelf for future reference. Whatever the coming days hold for her, mine has been the privilege of giving the girl three weeks of unclouded happiness.

Outside I hear the little Prince pacing up and down, yielding up his soul to holy meditations. I'd be willing to wager my best piece of jade his contemplations are something like a cycle from Nirvana, and closer far to a pair of heavily fringed eyes. Poor little imitation Buddha! He is grasping at the moon's reflection on the water. Somewhere near I hear Dolly's soft coo and deep-voiced replies. But unfinished packing, a bath and coffee are awaiting me.

Dawn is coming, and already through the port hole I see a dot of earth curled against the horizon. Above floats Fuji, the base wrapped in mists, the peak eternally white, a giant snowdrop swinging in a dome of perfect blue. The vision is a call to prayer, a wooing of the soul to the heights of undimmed splendor.

After all, Mate, I may give you and Jack a glad surprise and justify Sada handing me that letter addressed to a Christian Sister.

Yokohama, July, 1911.

Now that I am here, I am trying to decide what to do with myself. At home each day was so full of happy things and the happiest of all was listening for Jack's merry whistle as he opened the street door every night. At home there are always demands, big and little, popping in on me which I sometimes resent and yet being free from makes me feel as dismal as a long vacant house with the For Rent sign up, looks. In this Lotus land there is no *must* of any kind for the alien, and the only whistles I hear belong to the fierce little tugs that buzz around in the harbor, in and out among the white sails of the fishing fleet like big black beetles in a field of lilies. But you must not think life dull for me. Fate and I have cried a truce, and she is showing me a few hands she is dealing other people. But first listen to the tale I have to tell of the bruise she gave my pride this morning, that will show black for many a day.

I joined a crowd on the water's edge in front of the hotel to watch a funeral procession in boats. Recently a hundred and eighty fishermen were sent to the bottom by a big typhoon, and the wives and the sweethearts were being towed out to sea to pay a last tribute to them, by strewing the fatal spot with flowers and paper prayers. White-robed priests stood up in the front of the boats and chanted some mournful ritual, keeping time to the dull thumping of a drum. The air was heavy with incense. A dreamy melancholy filled the air and I thought how hallowed and beautiful a thing is memory. From out that silent watching crowd came a voice that sent my thoughts flying to starry nights of long ago and my first trip across the Pacific; soft south winds; vows of eternal devotion that kept time with the distant throbbing of a ship's engine. I fumed. I was facing little Germany and five littler Germanys strung out behind. You surely remember him? and how when I couldn't see things his way he swore to a wrecked heart and a never-to-be-forgotten constancy. Mate! There was no more of a flicker of memory in the stare of his round blue eyes than there would have been in a newly baked pretzel. I stood still, waiting for some glimmer of recognition. Instead, he turned to the pincushion on his arm, whom I took to be Ma O., and I heard him say "Herzallorliebsten." I went straight to the hotel and had it translated. Thought it had a familiar sound. Wouldn't it be interesting to know how many "only ones" any man's life history records? To think of my imagining him eating his heart out with hopeless longing in some far away Tibetan Monastery. And here he was, pudgy and content, with his fat little brood waddling along behind him. If our vision could penetrate the future, verily Romance would have to close up shop. Oh, no! I didn't want him to pine entirely away, but he needn't have been in such an everlasting hurry to get fat and prosperous over it. Wouldn't Jack howl?

I took good care to see that he was not stopping at this hotel. Then I went back to my own thoughts of the happy years that had been mine since Little Germany bade me a tearful good-by.

And, too, I wanted to think out some plan whereby I can keep in touch with Sada and be friendly with her relative.

Before I left the steamer, I had a surprise in the way of Uncles. Next time I will pause before I prophesy. But if Uncle was a blow to my preconceived ideas, I will venture Sada startled a few of his traditions as to nieces. Quarantine inspection was short, and when at last we cast anchor, the harbor was as blue as if a patch of the summer sky had dropped into it. The thatched roofs shone russet brown against the dark foliage of the hills. The temple roofs curved gracefully above the pink mist of the crêpe myrtle.

Sada was standing by me on the upper deck, fascinated by the picture. As she realized the long dreamed-of fairy-land

THE LADY AND SADA SAN

was unfolding before her, tears of joy filled her eyes and tears of another kind filled mine.

Sampans, launches and lighters clustered around the steamer as birds of prey gather to a feast: captains in gilt braid; coolies in blue and white, with their calling-cards stamped in large letters on their backs, and the story of their trade written around the tail of their coats in fantastic Japanese characters. Gentlemen in divided skirts and ladies in kimono and clogs swarmed up the gangway. In the smiling, pushing crowd I looked for the low-browed relative I expected to see. Imagine the shock, Mate, when a man with manners as beautiful as his silk kimono presented his card and announced that he was Uncle Mura. I had been pointed out as Sada's friend. A week afterwards I could have thought of something brilliant to say. Taken unawares, I stammered out a hope that his honorable teeth were well and his health poor. You see I am all right in Japanese if I do the talking. For I know what I want to say and what they ought to say. But when they come at me with a flank movement, as it were, I am lost. Uncle passed over my blunder without a smile and went on to say many remarkable things, if sound means anything. However, trust even a deaf woman to prick up her ears when a compliment is headed her way, whether it is in Sanskrit or Polynesian. In acknowledgment I stuck to my flag, and the man's command of quaint but correct English convinced me that I would have to specialize in something more than first thought if I was to cope with this tea-house proprietor whose armor is the subtle manners of the courtier.

Blessed Sada! Only the cocksureness of youth made her blind to the check her enthusiasm was meant to receive in the first encounter of the new life. She had always met people on equal terms, most men falling easy victims. She was blissfully ignorant that Mura, by directing his conversation to me, meant to convey to her that well-bred girls in this enchanted land lowered their eyes and folded their hands when they talked in the presence of a MAN, if they dared to talk at all.

Not so this half-child of the West. She fairly palpitated with joy and babbled away with the freedom of a sunny brook in the shadow of a grim forest. From the man's standpoint, he was not unkind; unrestraint was to him an incomprehensible factor in a young girl's make-up; and whatever was to follow, the first characters he meant her to learn must spell reverence and repression.

They hurried ashore to catch a train to Kioto. I must look harmless, for I was invited to call. I shall accept, for I have a feeling in spite of manners and silken robes that the day is not distant when the distress signals will be flying.

I waved good-by to the girl as the little launch made its way to land. She made a trumpet of her hands and called a merry "sayonara." The master of her future folded his arms and looked out to sea.

The next day I had a lonely lunch at the hotel. When I saw two lovery young things at the table where Jack and I had our wedding breakfast, so long ago, I made for the

THE LADY AND SADA SAN

other end of the room and persistently turned my back. But I saw out of the corner of my eye they were far away above food, and, Mate, believe me, they didn't even know it was hot, though a rain barrel couldn't have measured the humidity.

Of course Jack and I were much more sensible, but that whole blessed time is wrapped in rosy mists with streaks of moonlight to the tune of heavenly music, so it's futile to try to recall just what did happen. I ought to have gone to another hotel, but the chain of memory was too strong for me.

I was hesitating between the luxury of a sentimental spell and a fit of loneliness, when a happy interruption came in a message from Countess Otani, naming the next day at two for luncheon with her at the Arsenal Gardens at Tokio. How I wished for you, Mate! It was a fairy-story come true, dragons and all. The Arsenal Garden means just what it says. Only when the dove of peace is on duty are its gates opened, and then to but a few, high in command. For across the white-blossomed hedge that encloses the grounds, armies of men toil ceaselessly molding black bullets for pale people and they work so silently that the birds keep house in the long fringed willows and the goldfish splash in the sunned spots of the tiny lake.

After passing the dragons in the shape of sentries and soldiers, to each of whom I gave a brief life-history, I wisely followed my nose and a guard down the devious path.

The Countess received her guests in a banquet-hall all

ebony and gold, and was not seated permanently on a throne with a diamond crown screwed into her head as we used so fondly to imagine.

The simplicity of her hospitality was charming. She and most of her ladies-in-waiting had been educated abroad. But despite the lure of the Western freedom, they had returned to their country with their heads level and their traditions intact. But you guess wrong, honey, if you imagine custom and formality of official life have so overcome these high-born ladies as to make them lay figures who dare not raise their eyes except by rule. There were three American guests, and only by being as nimble as grasshoppers did we hold our own in the table talk which was as exhilarating as a game of snowball on a frosty day.

We scampered all around war and settled a few important political questions. Poetry, books and the new Cabinet vied with the merriment over comparisons in styles of dress. One delightful woman told how gloves and shoes had choked her when she first wore them in America. Another gave her experience in getting fatally twisted in her court train when she was making her bow before the German Empress.

A soft-voiced matron made us laugh over her story of how, when she was a young girl at a mission school, she unintentionally joined in a Christian prayer, and nearly took the skin off her tongue afterwards scrubbing it with strong soap and water to wash away the stain. There wasn't even a smile as she quietly spoke of the many times later

THE LADY AND SADA SAN

when with that same prayer she had tried to make less hard the after-horrors of war.

The possibilities of Japanese women are amazing even to one who thinks he knows them. They look as if made for decoration only, and with a flirt of their sleeves they bring out a surprise that turns your ideas a double somersault. Here they were, laughing and chatting like a bunch of fresh schoolgirls for whom life was one long holiday. Yet ten out of the number had recently packed away their gorgeous clothes, and laid on a high shelf all royal ranks and rights, for a nurse's dress and kit. Apparently delicate and shy they can be, if emergency demands, as grim as war or as tender as heaven.

It was a blithesome day and if it hadn't been for that "all gone" sort of a feeling, that possesses me when evening draws near and Jack is far away, content might have marked me as her own. As it was I put off playing a single at dinner as long as possible by calling on a month-old bride whom I had known as a girl. With glee I accepted the offer of an automobile to take me for the visit, and repented later. Two small chauffeurs and a diminutive footman raced me through the narrow, crowded streets, scattering the populace to any shelter it could find. The only reason we didn't take the fronts out of the shops is that Japanese shops are frontless. I looked back to see the countless victims of our speed. I saw only a crowd coming from cover, smiling with curiosity and interest. We hit the top of the hill with a flourish, and when I asked what was the hurry my attendants looked hurt and reproachfully asked if that wasn't the way Americans liked to ride.

Mate, this is a land of contrasts and contradictions. At the garden all had been life and color. At this home, where the wrinkled old servitor opened the heavily carved gates for me, it was as if I had stepped into a bit of ancient Japan, jealously guarded from any encroachment of new conditions or change of custom.

Like a curious package, contents unknown, I was passed from one automatic servant to another till I finally reached the *Torishimari* or mistress of ceremonies. By clock-work she offered me a seat on the floor, a fan and congratulations. This last simply because I was me. The house was ancient and beautiful. The room in which I sat had nothing in it but matting as fine as silk, a rare old vase with two flowers and a leaf in formal arrangement, and an atmosphere of aloofness that lulled mind and body to restful revery. After my capacity for tea and sugared dough was tested, the little serving maid fanning me, bowing every time I blinked, the paper doors near by divided noiselessly and, framed by the dim light, sat the young bride, quaint and oriental as if she had stepped out of some century-old kakemono. In contrast to my recent hostesses it was like coming from a garden of brilliant flowers into the soft, quiet shadows of a bamboo grove. No modern touch about this lady. She had been reduced by rule from a romping girl to a selfless creature fit for a Japanese gentleman's wife and no questions asked. Her hair, her dress, and even her speech were strictly by the laws laid down in a book for the thirty-first day of the first month after marriage. But I would like to see the convention with a crust thick enough to entirely obliterate one woman's interest in another whose clothes and life belong to a distant land. When I told her I had come to Japan against Jack's wishes and was going to follow him to China if I could, she paled at my rashness. How could a woman dare disobey? Would not my husband send me home, take my name off the house register and put somebody in my place?

Well now, wouldn't you like to see the scientist play any such tricks with me—that blessed old Jack who smiles at my follies, asks my advice, and does as he pleases, and for whom there has never been but the one woman in the world! I struggled to make plain to her the attitude of American men and women and the semi-independence of the latter. As well explain theology to a child. To her mind the undeviating path of absolute obedience was the only possible way. Anything outside of a complete renunciation of self-interest and thought meant ruin and was not even to be whispered about. I gave it up and came back to her sphere of poetry and mothers-in-law.

When I said good-by there was a gentle pity in her eyes, for she was certain her long-time friend was headed for the highroad of destruction. But instead I turned into the dim solitude of Shiba Park. I had something to think about. To-day's experiences had painted anew in naming colors the difference in husbands. How prone a woman is, who is free and dearly beloved, to fall into the habit of taking things for granted, forgetting how one drop of the full measure of happiness, that a good husband gives her, would turn to rosy tints the gray lives of hundreds of her kind who are wives in name only. Her appreciation may be abundant but it is the silent kind. Her bugaboo is fear of sentiment and when it is too late, she remembers with a heart-break.

I can think of a thousand things right now I want to say to Jack and while storing them away for some future happy hour, I walked further into the deep shadows of twilight.

Instantly the spell of the East was over me. Real life was not. In the soft green silences of mystery and fancy, I found a seat by an ancient moss-covered tomb. Dreamily I watched a great red dragon-fly frivol with the fairy blue wreaths of incense-smoke that hovered above the leaf shadows trembling on the sand. The deep melody of a bell, sifted through a cloud of blossom, caught up my willing soul and floated out to sea and Jack far from this lovely land, where stalks unrestrained the ugly skeleton of easy divorce for men. The subject always irritates me like prickly heat.

NIKKO, July, 1911.

Summer in Japan is no joke, especially if you are waiting for letters. I know perfectly well I can't hear from you

THE LADY AND SADA SAN

and Jack for an age, and yet I watch for the postman three times a day, as a hungry man waits for the dinner-bell.

The days in Yokohama were too much like a continuous Turkish bath, and I fled to Nikko, the ever moist and mossy. Two things you can always expect in this village of "roaring, wind-swept mountains,"—rain and courtesy. One is as inevitable as the other, and both are served in quantities.

I am staying in a semi-foreign hotel which is tucked away in a pocket in the side of a mountain as comfy as a fat old lady in a big rocker who glories in dispensing hospitality with both hands. Just let me put my head out of my room door and the hall fairly blossoms with little maids eager to serve. A step toward the entrance brings to life a small army of attendants bending as they come like animated jack-knives on a live wire. One struggles with the mystery of my overshoes, while the Master stands by and begs me to take care of my honorable spirit. As it is the only spirit I possess I heed his advice and bring it back to the hotel to find the entire force standing at attention, ready to receive me. I pass on to my room with a procession of bearers and bearesses strung out behind me like the tail of a kite, anything from a tea-tray to the sugar tongs being sufficient excuse for joining the parade.

When dressing for dinner, if I press the button, no less than six little picture maids flutter to my door, each begging for the honor of fastening me up the back. How delighted Jack would be to assign them this particular honor for life. Such whispers over the wonders of a foreign-made dress as they struggle with the curious fastenings! (They should hear my lord's fierce language!) Each one takes a turn till some sort of connection is made between hook and eye. All is so earnestly done I dare not laugh or wiggle with impatience. I may sail into dinner with the upper hook in the lower eye and the middle all askew, but the service is so graciously given, I would rather have my dress upside down than to grumble. Certainly I pay for it. I tip everything from the proprietor to the water-pitcher. But the sum is so disproportionate to the pleasure and the comfort returned that I smile to think of the triple price I have paid elsewhere and the high-nosed condescension I got in return for my money. Japanese courtesy may be on the surface, but the polish does not easily wear off and it soothes the nerves just as the rain cools the air. It goes without saying that I did not arrive in Nikko without a variety of experiences along the way.

Two hours out from Yokohama, the train boy came into the coach, and with a smile as cheerful as if he were saying, "Happy New Year," announced that there was a washout in front of us and a landslide at the back of us. Would everybody please rest their honorable bones in the village while a bridge was built and a river filled in. The passengers trailed into a settlement of straw roofs, bamboo poles and acres of white and yellow lilies. I went to a quaint little inn—that was mostly out!—built over a fussy brook; and a pine tree grew right out of the side of the house. My room was furnished with four mats and a poem hung on the wall. When the policeman came in to apologize for the rudeness of the storm in delaying me, the boy who brought my bags had to step outside so that the official would have room to bow properly. I ate my supper of fish-omelet and turnip pickle served in red lacquer bowls, and drank tea out of cups as big as thimbles. Jack says Japanese teacups ought to be forbidden; in a moment of forgetfulness they could so easily slip down with the tea.

It had been many a year since I was so separated from my kind and each hour of isolation makes clearer a thing I've never doubted, but sometimes forget, that the happiest woman is she whose every moment is taken up in being necessary to somebody; and to such, unoccupied minutes are like so many drops of lead. That, with a telegram I read telling of the increasing dangers of the plague in Manchuria, threatened to send me headlong into a spell of anxiety and the old terrible loneliness.

Happily the proprietor and his wife headed it off by asking me if I would be their guest for this evening to see the Bon Matsuri, the beautiful Festival of the Dead. On the thirteenth day of the seventh month, all the departed spirits take a holiday from Nirvana or any other seaport they happen to be in and come on a visit to their former homes to see how it fares with the living. Poor homesick spirits! Not even Heaven can compensate for the separation from beloved country and friends. As we passed along, the streets were alight with burning rushes placed at many doors to guide the spiritual excursionists. Inside, the people were praying, shrines were decorated and children in holiday dress merrily romped. Why, Mate, it was worth being a ghost just to come back and see how happy everybody was. For on this night of nights, cares and sorrows are doubly locked in a secret place and the key put carefully away. You couldn't find a coolie so heartless as to show a shadow of trouble to his ghostly relatives when they return for so brief a time to hold happy communion with the living. He may be hungry, he may be sick, but there is a brave smile of welcome on his lips for the spirits.

The crazy old temple at the foot of the mountain, glorified by a thousand lights and fluttering flags, reaped a harvest of *rins* and *sens* paid to the priests for paper prayers and bamboo flower-holders with which to decorate the graves. The cemetery was on the side of the hill, and every step of the way somebody stopped at a stone marker to fasten a lantern to a small fishing-pole and pin a prayer near by. This was to guide the spirit to his own particular spot.

A breeze as soft as a happy sigh came through the pines and gently rocked the lanterns. The dim figures of the worshipers moved swiftly about, as delighted as children in the shadow-pictures made by the twinkling lights, eagerly seeking out remote spots that no grave might be without its welcoming gleam. A long line of white-robed dancing girls came swaying by with clapping hands to soft-voiced chanting.

I, too, though an alien, was moved with the good-will

and kindness that sung through the very air and fearlessly I would have decorated any festive ghost that happened along. I looked to see where I might lay the offering I held in my hand. My hostess plucked my sleeve and pointed to a tiny tombstone under a camellia tree. I went closer and read the English inscription, "Dorothy Dale. Aged 2 years." There was a tradition that once in the long ago a missionary and his wife lived in the village. Through an awful epidemic of cholera they stuck to their posts, nursed and cared for the people. Their only child was the price they paid for their constancy. To each generation the story had been told, and through all the years faithful watch had been kept over the little enclosure. Now it was all a-glimmer with lanterns shaped like birds and butterflies. I added my small offering and turned hotelwards reluctantly.

My ancient host and hostess trotted along near by, eager to share all their pathetic little gaieties with me. Their lives together had about as much real comradeship as a small brown hen and a big gray owl, and they had been married sixty years! They had toiled and grown old together, but that did not mean that wifey was to walk anywhere but three feet to the rear, nor to speak except when her lord and ruler stopped talking to take a whiff of his pipe. I tried to walk behind with the old lady but she threatened to stand in one spot for the rest of the night. Then I vainly coaxed her to walk with me at her husband's side. But her face was so full of genuine horror at such disrespect that I desisted. Think, Mate, of trying to puzzle out the make-up of a nation which for the sake of a long-ago kindness will for years keep a strange baby's grave green and yet whose laws will divorce a woman for disobedience to her husband's mother and where the ancient custom of "women to heel" still holds good.

And this is the land where the Seeker came for the truth!

Sada thinks it paradise and I, as before, am sending to Jack

> A heart of love for thee
> Blown by the summer breezes
> Ten thousand miles of sea.

July, 1911.

Mate:

There ought to be some kind of capital punishment for the woman who has nothing to do but kill time. It's an occupation that puts crimps in the soul and offers the supreme moment in which the devil may work his rabbit foot. No, I cannot settle down or hustle up to anything until I hear from Jack or you. Very soon I will be reduced to doing the one desperate thing lurking in this corner of the woods, flirting with the solitary male guest, who has a strong halt in his voice and whose knees are not on speaking terms.

Of course it is raining. If the sun gets gay and tries

THE LADY AND SADA SAN

the bluff of being friendly, a heavy giant of a cloud rises promptly up from behind a mountain and puts him out of business. Still, why moan over the dampness? It makes the hills look like great green plush sofa-cushions and the avenues like mossy caves.

I have read till my eyes are crossed and I have written to every human I know. I have watched the giggling little maids patter up to a two-inch shrine and, flinging a word or two to Buddha, use the rest of their time to gossip. And the old lady who washes her vegetables and her clothes in the same baby-lake just outside my window amuses me for at least ten minutes. Then, Mate, for real satisfaction, I must turn to you, whose patience is elastic and enduring. It is one of my big joys that your interest and love are just the same, as in those other days when you packed me off to Japan for the good of my country and myself; and then sent Jack after me. Guess I should have stayed at home, as Jack told me, but I am glad I did not.

Though it has poured every minute I have been here, there have been bursts of sunshine inside, if not out. The other day my table boy brought me the menu and asked for an explanation of *assorted* fruits. I told him very carefully it meant *mixed, different kinds*. He is a smart lad. He understands my Japanese! He grasped my meaning immediately, and wrote it down in a little book. This morning he came to my room and announced: "Please, Lady, some assorted guests await you in the audience chamber; one Japanese and two American persons."

I have had my first letter from Sada too, simply spilling over with youth and enthusiasm. The girl is stark mad over the fairy-landness of it all. Says her rooms are in Uncle's private house, which is in quite a different part of the garden from the tea-house. (Thank the Lord for small mercies!) She says Uncle has given her some beautiful clothes and is so good to her. I dare say. He has taken her to see a lovely old castle and wonderful temple. The streets are all pictures and the scenery is glorious! That is true, but the girl cannot live off scenery any more than a nightingale can thrive on the scent of roses. What is coming when the glamour of the scenery wears off and Uncle puts on the pressure of his will?

I have not dared to give her any suggestion of warning. She is deadly sure of her duty, so enthralled is she with the thought of service to her mother's people. If I am to help her, the shock of disillusionment must come from some other direction. The *disillusioner* is seldom forgiven. I do not know what plans are being worked out behind Uncle's lowered eyelids. But I *do* know his idea of duty does not include keeping such a valuable asset as a bright and beautiful niece hid away for his solitary joy. In fact, he would consider himself a neglectful and altogether unkind relative if he did not marry Sada off to the very best advantage to himself. In the name of all the Orient, what else is there to do with a *girl*, and especially one whose blood is tainted with that of the West?

Well, Mate, my thoughts grew so thick on the subject

THE LADY AND SADA SAN

I nearly suffocated. I went for a walk and ran right into a cavalcade of donkeys, jinrickshas and chairs, headed by the Seeker and Dolly, who has also annexed the little Maharajah.

They had been up to Chuzenji—and Chuzenji I would have you know is lovely enough, with its emerald lake and rainbow mists, to start a man's tongue to love-making whether he will or not. And so surely as it is raining, something has happened. Dolly was as gay as a day-old butterfly and smiled as if a curly-headed Cupid had tickled her with a wing-feather. The Seeker was deadly solemn. Possibly the aftermath of his impetuosity.

Oh, well! there is no telling what wonders can be worked by incurable youthfulness and treasures laid up in a trust company.

The little Prince, with every pocket and his handkerchief full of small images of Buddha which he was collecting, asked at once for Sada. His heart was in his eyes, but there is no use tampering with a to-be-incarnation by encouraging worldly thoughts. So I said I had not seen her since we landed. They were due on board the "Siberia" in Yokohama to-night on their way to China. I waved them good wishes and went on, amused and not a little troubled. Worried over Sada, hungry for Jack, lonesome for you. I passed one of the gorgeous blue, green and yellow gates, at the entrance of a temple. On one side is carved a distorted figure, that looks like a cross between an elephant and a buzzard. It is called "Baku, the eater of evil dreams." My word! but I could furnish him a feast that would give him the fanciest case of indigestion he ever knew!

Mate, you would have to see Nikko, with its majestic cryptomarias, sheltering the red and gold lacquer temples; you would have to feel the mystery of the gray-green avenues, and have its holy silences fall like a benediction upon a restless spirit, to realize what healing for soul and body is in the very air, to understand why I joyfully loitered for two hours and came back sane and hungry, but wet as a fish.

Write me about the only man, the kiddies and your own blessed happy self.

I agree with Charity. "Ef you want to spile a valuable wife, tu'n her loose in a patch of idlesomeness."

Still at Nikko, August, 1911.

You beloved girl, I have heard from Jack and my heart is singing a ragtime tune of joy and thanksgiving. How he laughed at me for being too foolishly lonesome to stay in America without him. Oh, these, men! Does he forget he raged once upon a time, when he was in America without me? As long as I am here though, he wants me to have as good a time as possible. Do anything I want, and—blessed trusting man!—buy anything I see that will fit in the little house at home.

Can you believe it? After a fierce battle the sun won out

THE LADY AND SADA SAN

this morning, and even the blind would know by the dancing feel of the air that it was a glorious day. At eight o'clock, when the little maids went up to the shrine, happy as kittens let out for a romp, they forgot even to look Buddhaward and took up their worship time in playing tag. The old woman who uses the five-foot lake as the family washtub, brought out all her clothes, the grand-baby, and the snub-nosed poodle that wears a red bib, to celebrate the sunshine by a carnival of washing.

I could not stand four walls a minute longer. I am down in the garden writing you, in a tea-house made with three fishing-poles and a bunch of straw. It is covered with pink morning-glories as big as coffee cups.

It has been three weeks since my last letter and I know your interest in Jack and germs is almost as great as mine. Jack has been in Peking. He thinks the revolution of the Chinese against the Manchu Government is going to be something far more serious this time than a flutter of fans and a sputter of shooting-crackers. The long-suffering worm with the head of a dragon is going to turn, and when it does, there will not be a Manchu left to tell the pig tale.

Jack is in Mukden now, where he is about to lose his mind with joy over the prospect of looking straight in the eye—if it has one—this wicked old germ with a new label, and telling it what he thinks. The technical terms he gives are as paralyzing as a Russian name spelled backwards.

In a day's time this fearful thing wipes out entire families and villages. It has simply ravaged northern Manchuria and the country about. Jack says so deadly are the effects of these germs in the air that if a man walking along the street happens to breathe in one, he is a corpse on the spot before he is through swallowing. The remains are gathered up by men wearing shrouds and net masks, and the peaceful Oriental who was not doing a thing but attending strictly to his own business, is soon reduced to ashes. All because of a pesky microbe with a surplus of energy.

You know perfectly well, Mate, Jack does not speak in this frivolous manner of his beloved work. The interpretation is wholly mine. But I dare not be serious over it. I must push any thought of his danger to the further ends of nowhere.

Jack thinks the native doctors have put up a brave fight, but so far the laugh has been all on the side of the frisky germ.

It blasts everything it touches and is most fastidious. Nobody can blame it for choosing as its nesting-place the little soft furred Siberian marmots, which the Chinese hunt for their skin. If only the hunters could be given a dip in a sulphur vat before they lay them down to sleep in the unspeakable inns with their spoils wrapped around them, the chance for infection would not be so great. Of course the bare suggestion of a bath might prove more fatal than the plague, for oftener than not the hunters are used only as a method of travel by the merry microbe and are immune from the effects. Of course Jack has all sorts of theories as to why this is so. But did you ever see a scientist

THE LADY AND SADA SAN

who didn't have a workable theory for everything from the wrong end of a carpet-tack to the evolution of a June bug?

From the hunters and their spoils the disease spreads and their path southwards can be traced by desolated villages and piles of bones.

Jack tells me he is garbed in a long white robe effect (I hope he won't grow wings), with a good-sized mosquito net on a frame over his head and face. He works in heavy gloves. Mouth and nose being the favorite point of attack, everybody who ventures out wears over this part of the face a curiously shaped shield, whose firm look says, "No admittance here." But all the same, that germ from Siberia is a wily thief and steals lives by the thousands, in spite of all precautions.

Jack is as enthusiastic over the fight against the scourge as a college boy over football. His letter has so many big technical words in it, I had to pay excess postage.

I've read his letter twice, but to save me I cannot find any suggestion of the remotest possibility of my coming nearer. Yes, I know I said Japan only. But way down in the cellar of my heart I *hoped* he would say nearer.

What a happy day it has been. Here is your letter, just come. The priests up at the temple have asked me to see the ceremony of offering food to the spirits, in the holy of holies.

There is not time for me to add another word to this letter. What a dear you are, to love while you lecture me. What you say is all true. A woman's place *is* in her home.

But just now out of the East, I've had a call to play silent partner to science and while it's a lonesome sport, at least it's far more entertaining than caring for a husbandless house. Anyhow I am sending you a hug and a thousand kisses for the babies.

SHOJI LAKE, August, 1911.

Mate, think of the loveliest landscape picture you ever saw, put me in it and you will know where I am. With some friends from Honolulu and a darling old man—observe I say *old*!—from Colorado, we started two days ago, to walk around the base of Fuji. Everything went splendidly till a typhoon hit us amidships and sent us careening, blind, battered and soaked into this red and white refuge of a hotel, that clings to the side of a mountain like a woodpecker to a telephone pole. I have seen storms, but the worst I ever saw was a playful summer breeze compared with the magnificent fury of this wind that snapped great trees in two as if they had been young bean-poles, and whipped the usually peaceful lake into raging waves that swept through a gorge and greedily licked up a whole village.

Our path was high up, but right over the water. Sometimes we were crawling on all fours. Mostly we were flying just where the wind listed. If a tree got in our way as we flew, so much the worse for us. It is funny now, but it was not at the time! Seriously, I was in immediate peril of

THE LADY AND SADA SAN

being blown to glory *via* the fierce green foam below. My Colorado Irishman is not only a darling, but a hero. Once I slipped, and stopped rolling only when some faithful pines were too stubborn to let go.

I was many feet below the reach of any arm. In a twinkling, my friend had stripped the kimono off the baggage coolie's back, and made a lasso with which he pulled me up. Then shocked to a standstill by the shortcomings of the coolie's birthday suit, he snatched off his coat and gave it to him, with a dollar. Such a procession of bedraggled and exhausted pleasure-seekers as we were, when three men stood behind our hotel door and opened it just wide enough to haul us in. But hot baths and boiling tea revived us and soon we were as merry as any people can be who have just escaped annihilation.

The typhoon passed as suddenly as it came, and now the world—or at least this part of it—is as glowing and beautiful as if freshly tinted by the Master Hand.

A moment ago I looked up to see my rescuer gazing out of the window. I asked, "How do you feel, Mr. Carson?" His voice trembled when he answered: "Lady, I feel glorified, satisfied and nigh about petrified. Look at that!"

Below lay Shoji, its shimmering waters rimmed with velvety green. Every raindrop on the pines was a prism; the mountain a brocade of blossom. To the right Fuji, the graceful, ever lovely Fuji; capricious as a coquette and bewitching in her mystery, with a thumbnail moon over her peak, like a silver tiara on the head of a proud beauty; at her base the last fleecy clouds of the day, gathered like worshipers at the feet of some holy saint.

The man's face shone. For forty years he had worked at harness-making, always with the vision before him that some day he might take this trip around the world. He has the soul of an artist, which has been half starved in the narrow environment of his small town life. Cannot you imagine the mad revel of his soul in this pictureland?

He is going to Mukden. Of course I told him all about Jack's work. The old fellow, he must be all of seventy, was thrilled. I am going to give him a letter to Jack. Also to some friends in Peking; they will be good to him. If anybody deserves a merry-go-round sort of a holiday, he does. Think of sewing on saddles and bridles all these years, when his heart was withering for beauty!

I am glad of your eager interest in Sada. How like you! Never too absorbed in your own life to share other people's joys and sorrows and festivities.

If your wise head evolves a plan of action, send by wireless, for if I read aright her message received to-day, the time is fast coming when the red lights of danger will be flashing. I will quote: "Last night Uncle asked me to sing to some people who were giving a dinner at the tea-house. I put on my loveliest kimono and a hair-dresser did my hair in the old Japanese style and stuck a red rose at the side. For the first time I went into that beautiful, *beautiful* place my Uncle calls 'the Flower Blooming' tea-house. It was more like a fairy palace. How the girls, who live

THE LADY AND SADA SAN

there, laughed at my guitar. They had never seen one before. How they whispered over the color of my eyes. Said they matched my kimono, and they tittered over my clumsiness in sitting on the floor. But I forgot everything when the door slid open and I looked into the most wonderful dream-garden that ever was, and people everywhere. I finished singing, there was clapping and loud *banzais*. I looked up and realized there were *only* men at this dinner and I never saw so many bottles in all my life. I felt very strange and so far away from dear Susan West. After I had sung once more I started back to my home. Uncle met me. I told him I was going to bed. For the first time he was cross and ordered me back to the play place, where I was to stay until he came for me. There never was anything so lovely as the green and pink garden and the lily-shaped lights, and the flowers; and such *pretty* girls who knew just what to do. But I cannot understand the men who come here. When dear old Billy"—thank heaven she says *dear* Billy!—"talks I know just what he means. But these men use so many words Susan never taught me, and laugh so loud when they say them.

"There was one man named Hara whose clothes were simply gorgeous. The girls say he is very rich, and a great friend of Uncle's! He may have money, but he is not overburdened with manners. He can out-stare an owl."

There was more. But that is enough to show me Uncle's hand as plainly as if I were a palmist. If nothing happens to prevent, the man promises to do what thousands of his kind have done before: regardless of obstacles and consequences marry the girl off to the highest bidder; rid himself of all responsibility and make a profit at the same time. From his point of view it is the only thing to do. He would be the most astonished uncle in Mikado-land if anybody suggested to him that Sada had any rights or feelings in the matter. He would tell you that as Sada's only male relative, custom gave him the right to dispose of her as he saw fit, and custom is law and there is nothing back of *that!*

So far I have played only a thinking part in the drama. But I will not stand by and see the girl, whose very loneliness is a plea, sacrificed without some kind of a struggle to help her. At the present writing I feel about as effective as a February lamb, and every move calls for tact. Wish I had been born with a needle wit instead of a Roman nose! For if Uncle has a glimmer of a suspicion that I would befriend Sada at the cost of his plans, so surely as the river is lost in the sea, Sada would disappear from my world until it was too late for me to lend a hand.

Good-by, Mate. At eventide, as of old, look my way and send me strength from your vast store of calm courage and common sense. The odds are against me, but the god of luck has never yet failed to laugh with me.

September, 1911.

I am in a monastery, Mate, but only temporarily, thank

THE LADY AND SADA SAN

you. It is a blessing to the cause that Fate did not turn me into a monk or a sister or any of those inconvenient things with a restless religion, that wakes you up about 3 A. M. on a wintry dawn to pray shiveringly to a piece of wood, to the tune of a thumping drum. Some morning when the frost was on the cypress that carven image would disappear!

For one time at least I would have a nice fire, and my prayers would not be decorated with icicles.

For two weeks my friends and I have been tramping through picture-book villages and silk-worm country, and over mountain winding ways, sleeping on the floor, sitting on our feet and giving our stomachs surprise parties with hot, cold and lukewarm rice, seaweed and devil-fish.

It has been one hilarious lark of outdoor life, with nothing to pin us to earth but the joy of being a part of so beautiful a world.

The road led us through superb forests, over the Bridge of Paradise to Koyo San, whose peak is so far above the mist-wreathed valleys that it scrapes the clouds as they float by. But I want to say right here; Kobo Daishi, who founded this monastery in the distant ages and built a temple to his own virtues, may have been a saint, but he was not much of a gentleman! Else he would not have been so reckless of the legs and necks of the coming generations, as to blaze the trail to his shrine over mountains so steep that our pack-mule coming up could easily have bitten off his own tail if he had so minded.

Later.

This afternoon I must hustle down. I suppose the only way to get down is to roll. Well; anyway I am in a hurry. My mail beat me up the trail and a letter from Sada San begs me to come to Kioto to see her as soon as I can. She only says she needs help and does not know what to do. And blessed be the telegram that winds up from Hiroshima; the school is in urgent need of an assistant at the Kindergarten and they ask me to come. The principal, Miss Look, has gone to America on business, for three months. Hooray! Here is my chance to resign from the "Folded Hands' Society" and do something that is really worth while, as long as I cannot go to my man. How good it will seem once again to be in that dear old mission school, where in the long ago I toiled and laughed and suffered while I waited for Jack.

The prospect of being with the girls and the kiddies again makes me want to do a Highland Fling, even if I am in a monastery with a sad-faced young priest serving me tea and mournful sighs between prayers.

What a flirtatious old world it is after all. It smites you and bruises you, then binds up the hurts by giving you a desire or so of your heart. Just now the desire of my heart is to catch that train for Kioto.

So here goes a prayer, pinned to a shrine, for a body intact as I tread the path that drops straight down the mountain,

THE LADY AND SADA SAN

through the crimson glory of the maples and the blazing yellow of the gingko tree, to the tiny little station far away that looks like a decorated hen-coop.

Kioto, September, 1911.

Dearest Mate:

I cannot spend a drop of ink in telling you how I got here. How the baggage beast ran away and decorated the mountain shrubbery with my belongings. And how after all my hurry of dropping down from Koyo San, the brakesman forgot to hook our car to the train and started off on a picnic while the engine went merrily on and left us out in the rice-fields. Suffice it to say I landed in a whirl that spun me down to Uncle's house and back to the hotel. And by the way my thoughts are going, for all I know I may be booked to spin on through eternity.

My visit to Sada was so full of things that did not happen. When I reached the house, I sent in my card to Sada. Uncle came gliding in like a soft-footed panther. He did it so quietly that I jumped when I saw him. We took up valuable time repeating polite greetings, as set down on page ten of the Book of Etiquette, in the chapter on Calls Made by Inconvenient Foreigners.

When our countless bows were finished, I asked in my coaxingest voice if I might see Sada. Presently she came in, dressed in Japanese clothes and beautiful even in her pallor. She was changed—sad, and a little drooping. The conflict of her ideals of duty to her mother's people and the real facts in the case, had marked her face with something far deeper than girlish innocence. It was inevitable. But above the evidences of struggle there was a something which said the dead and gone Susan West had left more than a mere memory. Silently I blessed all her kind.

Sada was unfeignedly glad to see me, and I longed to take her in my arms and kiss her. But such a display would have marked me in Uncle's eyes as a dangerous woman with unsuppressed emotions, and unfit for companionship with Sada. I had hoped his Book of Etiquette said, "After this, bow and depart." But my hopes had not a pin-feather to rest on. He stayed right where he was. All right, old Uncle, thought I, if stay you will, then I shall use all a woman's power to beguile you and a woman's wit to out-trick you, so I can make you show your hand. It is going to be a game with the girl as the prize. It is also going to be like playing leap-frog with a porcupine. He has cunning and authority to back him, and I have only my love for Sada.

For a time I talked at random, directing my whole conversation to him as the law demands. By accident, or luck, I learned that the weak point in his armor of polite reserve was color prints. Just talk color prints to a collector and you can pick his pocket with perfect ease.

My knowledge of color prints could be written on my thumb nail. But I made a long and dangerous shot, by looking wise and asking if he thought Matahei compared favorably with Moronobo as painters of the same era. I choked off a gasp when I said it, for I would have you know that for all I knew, Matahei might have lived in the time of Jacob and Rebecca, and Moronobo a thousand years afterwards. But I guessed right the very first time and Mura San, with a flash of appreciation at my interest, said that my learning was remarkable. It was an untruth and he knew that I knew it, but it was courteous and I looked easy. Then he talked long and delightfully as only lovers of such things can. At least, it would have been delightful had I not been so anxious to see Sada alone. But it was not to be. At least, not then. But mark one for me, Mate: Uncle was so pleased with my keen and hungry interest in color prints and my desire to see his collection, that he invited me to a feast and a dance at the house the next night.

The following evening I could have hugged the person, male or otherwise, who called my dear host away for a few minutes just before the feast began.

Sada told me hurriedly that Uncle had insisted on her singing every night at the tea-house. She had first rebelled, and then flatly refused, for she did not like the girls. She hated what she saw and was afraid of the men. Her master was furiously angry; said he would teach her what obedience meant in this country. He would marry her off right away and be rid of a girl who thought her foreign religion gave her a right to disobey her relatives. She was afraid he would do it, for he had not asked her to go to the tea-house again. Neither had he permitted her to go out of the house. Once she was sick with fear, for she knew Uncle had been in a long consultation with the rich man Hara and he was in such good humor afterwards. But Hara, she learned, had gone away.

She would *not* sing at these dinners again, not if Uncle choked her and what must she do! I saw the man returning but I quickly whispered, "What about Billy?"

Ah, I knew I was right. The rose in her hair was no pinker than her cheeks. If Billy could only have seen her then, I would wager my shoes—and shoes are precious in this country—that her duty to her mother's people would have to take a back seat.

Before Uncle reached us I whispered, "Keep Billy in your heart, Sada. Write him. Tell him." And in the same breath I heartily thanked Uncle for inviting me.

It *was* a feast, Mate—the most picturesque, uneatable feast I ever sat on my doubly honorable feet to consume. There were opal-eyed fish with shaded pink scales, served whole; soft brown eels split up the back and laid on a bed of green moss; soups, thin and thick; lotus root and mountain lily, and raw fish. Each course—and their name was many—was served on a little two-inch-high lacquer table, with everything to match. Sometimes it was gold lacquer, then again green, once red and another black. But it was all a dream of color that shaded in with the little maids who served it; and they, swift, noiseless and pretty, were trained to graceful perfection. The few furnishings of the room were priceless. Uncle sat by in his silken robes, gracious and courteous, surprising me with his knowledge of current events. In the guise of host, he is charming. That is, if only he would not always talk with dropped eyelids, giving the impression that he is half dreaming and is only partly conscious of the world and its follies. And all the time I know perfectly well that he sees everything around him and clean on to the city limits.

Again and again in his talks he referred to his color prints and the years of patience required to collect them. Right then, Mate, I made a vow to study the pesky things as they have seldom been attacked before—even though I never had much use for pictures in which you cannot tell the top side from the bottom, without a label. But then, Jack says, my artistic temperament will never keep me awake at night. Now I decided all at once to make a collection. Heaven knows what I will do with it. But Uncle grew so enthusiastic he included his niece in the conversation, and while his humor was at high tide I coaxed him into a promise that Sada might come down to Hiroshima very soon, and help me look for prints.

Yes, indeed there was a dance afterwards, and everything was deadly, hysterically solemn—so rigidly proper, so stiffly conventional that it palled. It was the most maleless house of revelry I ever saw. Why, even the kakemono were pictures of perfect ladies and the gate-man was a withered old woman.

There was absolutely nothing wrong I could name. It was all exquisitely, daintily, lawfully Japanese. But I sat by my window till early morning. There was a very ghost of a summer moon. Out of the night came the velvety tones of a mighty bell; the sing-song prayers of many priests; the rippling laugh of a little child and the tinkling of a samisen. Every sound made for simple joy and peace. But I thought of the girl somewhere beyond the twinkling street lights, who, with mixed races in her blood and a strange religion in her heart, had dreamed dreams of this as a perfect land, and was now paying the price of disillusionment with bitter tears.

Eight o'clock the next morning.

I cabled Jack, "Hiroshima for winter."
He answered, "Thank the Lord you are nailed down at last."
P.S.—I have bought all the books on color prints I could find.

October, 1911.

Hiroshima! Get up and salute, Mate! Is not that name like the face of an old familiar friend? I have to shake myself to realize that it is not the long ago, but *now*. A recent picture of Jack and one of you and the babies is about the only touch of the present. Everything is just as it was in

THE LADY AND SADA SAN

the old days, when the difficulties of teaching in a foreign kindergarten in a *foreigner* language was the least of the battle that faced me. Well, I thought I'd finished with battles, but there's a feeling of fight in the air.

Same little room, in the same old mission school. Same wall paper, so blue it turned green. And, Lord love us, from the music-rooms still come the sounds like all the harmonies of a baby organ-factory gone on a strike.

But bless you, honey, there is an eternity of difference in having to stand a thing and doing it of your own free will. As Black Charity would remark, "I don't pay 'em no mind," and let them wheeze out their mournful complaints to the same old hymns.

Had you been here the night my dinky little train pulled into the station, you would have guessed that it was a big Fourth of July celebration or the Emperor's birthday. I would not dare guess how many girls there were to meet me. It seemed like half a mile of them lined up on the platform, and each carried a round red lantern.

Until they had made the proper bow with deadly precision, there was not a smile or a sound. That ceremony over, they charged down upon me in an avalanche of gaiety. They waved their lanterns, they called *banzai*, they laughed and sung some of the old time foolish songs we used to sing. They promptly put to rout all legends of their excessive modesty and shyness. They were just young and girlish. Plain happy. Eager and sweet in their generous welcome. It warmed every fiber of my being. When they thinned out a little, I saw at the other end of the platform a figure flying towards me, with the sleeves of her kimono out-stretched like the wings of a gray bird, and a great red rose for a top-knot. It was Miss First River, a little late, but more than happy, as she sobbed out her welcome on the front of my clean shirt-waist.

It was she, you remember, who in all those other years was my faithful secretary and general comforter. The one who slept across my door when I was ill and who never forgot the hot water bag on a cold night. For years she has supported a drunken father and a crazy mother; has sent one brother to America and made a preacher of another.

Now she is to be married, she told me in a little note she slipped into my hand as we walked up the Street of the Upper Flowing River to the school, adding, "Please guess my heart."

And miracle of the East! She has known the man a long time and they are in love! I am so glad I am going to be here for the wedding. It comes off in a few weeks.

I started work in the kindergarten this morning. It has been said that when the Lord ran out of mothers he made kindergartners. Surely he never did a better job—for the kindergartners. Mate, when I stepped into that room, it was like going into an enchanted garden of morning-glories and dahlias. What a greeting the regiment of young Japlings gave me! I just drank in all the fragrance of joy in the eager comradeship and sweet friendliness of the small Mikados and Mikadoesses with a keen delight that made the hours spin like minutes.

And would you believe it? The first sound that greeted my ears after their whole duty had been accomplished in the very formal bow, was—"Oh—it is the *skitten Sensei* (skipping teacher) A skit! A skit! We want to skit!" Of course, they were not the same children by many years. But things die slowly in Hiroshima. Even good reputations. Everything was pushed aside, and work or no work, teachers and children celebrated by one mad revel of skipping.

There are many things to do, and getting into the old harness of steady routine work and living on the tap of a bell, is not so easy as it sounds, after years of live-as-you-please. But it is good for the constitution and is satisfying to the soul.

I once asked my friend Carson from Colorado if he could choose but one gift in all the world, what would it be? "The contintment of stidy work," answered the wise old philosopher from out of the West; and my heart echoes his wisdom.

Had a big fat letter from Jack, and the reputation he gives those germs he is associating with, is simply disgraceful. He gives me statistics also. Wish he wouldn't. It takes so much time and I always have to count on my fingers.

He tells me, too, of an English woman who has joined the insect expedition. Says she is the most brilliant woman he ever met. Thanks awfully. And he has to sit up nights studying, to keep up with her. I dare say.

I'll wager she's high of color and mighty of muscle and

with equal vehemence says a thing is "strawdn'ry" whether it's a dewdrop or a spouting volcano.

I can't help feeling a little bit envious of her—out there with my Jack! Well! I will not get agitated till I have to.

A note from Sada says Uncle has had another outburst. He still consents for her to come down here. Her beautiful ideals have been smashed to smithereens, and the fact that nothing has ever been invented that will stick them together, adds no comfort to the situation. Her disappointment is heart-breaking. I cannot make a move till I get her to myself and have a life-and-death talk with her. I am playing for time.

I wrote her a cheerfully foolish letter. Told her I was making all kinds of plans for her visit. I also looked up some doubtful dates—at least, my textbook on color prints said they were doubtful—and referred them to Uncle for confirmation, asking that he give instructions to Sada about a certain dealer in Hiroshima who has some pictures so violent, positively I would not hang them in the cowshed. That is, if I cared for Suky. But it is anything for conversation now.

I almost forgot to tell you that we have the same *chef* as when I was kindergarten teacher here in the school years ago. He's prosperous as a pawnbroker. He gave me a radiant greeting. "How are you, *Tanaka?*" quoth I. "All same like damn monkey, *Sensei*," he replied. But he is unfailingly cheerful and the cleverest grafter in the universe, with an artistic temperament highly developed; he sometimes sends in the unchewable roast smothered in cherry blossoms.

How wise you were, Mate, to choose home and husband instead of a career. I love you for it.

HIROSHIMA, October, 1911.

For springing surprises, all full of kindness and delicate courtesies, Japanese girls would be difficult to equal. Before a whisper of it reached me, they made arrangements the other day for a re-union of all my graduates of the kindergarten normal class. It is hard to imagine when they found the time for the elaborate decorations they put up in the big kindergarten room, and the hundred and one little things they had done to show their love and warmth of welcome. It was a part of their play to blindfold me and lead me in. When I opened my eyes, there they stood. Twenty-five happy faces smiling into mine, and twenty babies to match. It was the kiddies that saved the day. I was not a little bewildered, and tears stung my eyes. But with one accord the babies set up a howl at anything so inconceivable as a queer foreign thing with a tan head appearing in their midst. When peace was restored by natural methods, the fun began.

The girls fairly bombarded me with questions. Could I come to see every one of them? Where was Jack? Could they see his picture? Did he say I could come? How "glad" it was to be together again. Did I remember how we used to play? Then everybody giggled. One thought had touched them all. Why not play now!

The baby question was quickly settled. Soon there was a roaring fire in my study. We raided the classroom for rugs and cushions and with the collection made down beds in a half ring around the crackling flames. On each we put a baby, feet fireward. We called in the *Obasan* (old woman) to play nurse, and on the table near we placed a row of bottles marked "First aid to the hungry." As I closed the door of the emergency nursery, I looked back to see a semi-circle of pink heels waving hilariously. Surely the fire goddess never had lovelier devotees than the Oriental cherubs that lay cooing and kicking before it that day.

How we played! In all the flowery kingdom so many foolish people could not have been found in one place. What chaff and banter! What laying aside of cares, responsibilities, and heavy hearts, if there were any, and just being free and young! For a time at least the years fell away from us and we relived all the games and folk-dances we ever knew. True, time had stiffened joints and some of the movements were about as graceful as a pair of fire tongs and I may be dismissed for some of the fancy steps I showed the girls, but they were happy, and far more supple than when we began.

When we were breathless we hauled in our old friend the big hibachi, with a peck of glowing charcoal right in the middle. We sat on our folded feet and made a big circle all around, with only the glimmer of the coals for a light. Then we talked.

Each girl had a story to tell, either of herself or some one we had known together. Over many we laughed. For others the tears started.

Warmed by companionship and moved by unwonted freedom, how much the usually reserved women revealed of themselves, their lives, their trials and desires! But whatever the story, the dominant note was acceptance of what was, without protest. It may be fatalism, Mate, but it is indisputable that looking finality in the face had brought to all of them a quietness of spirit that no longing for wider fields or personal ambition can disturb.

None of them had known their husbands before marriage. Few had ever seen them. Many were compelled to live with the difficulties of an exacting mother-in-law, who had forgotten that she was ever a young wife.

But above it all there was a cheerful peacefulness; a willingness of service to the husband and all his demands, a joy in children and home, that was convincing as to the depth and dignity of character which can so efface itself for the happiness of others.

One girl, Miss Deserted Lobster Field, was missing. I asked about her and this is her story. She was quite pretty; when she left school there was no difficulty in marrying her off. Two months afterward the young husband left to serve his time in the army. For some reason the mother-in-law did not "enter into the spirit of the girl," and without consulting those most concerned, she divorced her son and sent the girl home. When the soldier-husband returned, a new wife, whom he had never seen, was waiting for him at the cottage door.

The sent-home wife was terribly in the way in her father's house, for by law she belonged neither there nor in any other place. It is difficult to re-marry these offcasts. Something, however, had to be done. So dear father took a stroll out into the village, and being sonless adopted a young boy as the head of his house. A *yoshi* this boy is called. Father married the adopted son to the soldier's wife that was, securely and permanently. A yoshi has no voice in any family matter and is powerless to get a divorce.

Moral: If in Japan you want to make sure of keeping a husband when you get him, take a boy to raise, then marry him.

But the wedding of weddings is the one which took place last summer, by suggestion. The great unseen has lived in America for two years. The maid makes her home in the school. The groom-to-be wrote to a friend in Hiroshima: "Find me a wife." The friend wrote back: "Here she is." Miss Chestnut Tree, the maid, fluttered down to the courthouse, had her name put on the house register of the faraway groom, did up her hair as a married woman should and went back to work.

To-morrow she sails for America, and we are all going down to wave her good-by and good luck.

She is married all right. There will be no further

ceremony.

I would not dare tell you all the stories they told me. For I would never stop writing and you would never stop laughing or crying.

The end of all things comes sometimes. The beautiful afternoon ended too soon. But for the rest of time, this day will be crowned with halos made with the mightiness of the love and the dearness of the girls who were once my students, always my friends.

It took some time to assort the babies and make sure of tying the right one on the right mother's back. Not by one shaved head could I see the slightest difference in any of them, but mothers have the knack of knowing.

Out of the big gate they went and down the street all aglow with the early evening lights twinkling in the purple shadows. Their *geta* click-clacked against the hard street, to the music of their voices as they called back to me, "*Oyasumi, Oyasumi, Go kigen yoro shiku*" (Honorably rest. Be happy always to yourself).

My gratitude to this little country is great, Mate. It has given me much. It was here life taught me her sternest lessons. And here I found the heart's-ease of Jack's love. But for nothing am I more thankful than for the love and friendship of the young girl-mothers who were my pupils, but from whom I have learned more of the sweetness and patience of life than I could ever teach.

November, 1911.

Mate, there is a man in Hiroshima for whom I long and watch as I do for no other inhabitant. It is the postman. You should see him grin as he trots around the corner and finds me waiting at the gate, just as I used to do in the old teaching days. I doubly blest him this morning. Thank you for your letter. It fairly sings content. Homeyness is in every pen stroke.

Please say to your small son David that I will give his love to the "king's little boy" *if* I see him. My last glimpse of him was in Nikko. Poor little chap. He was permitted to walk for a moment. In that moment he spied a bantam hen, the anxious mother of half a dozen puff-ball chickens. Royalty knew no denial and went in pursuit. The bantam knew no royalty, pursued also. The four men and six women attendants were in a panic. The baby was rescued from a storm of feathers and taken back to the palace with an extra guard of three policemen.

I have been very busy, at play and at work. We have just had a wedding tea. My former secretary, Miss First River, as she expressed it, "married with" Mr. East Village.

The wedding took place at the ugly little mission church, which was transformed into a beautiful garden, with weeping willows, chrysanthemums, and mountain ferns. Also we had a wedding-bell. In a wild moment of enthusiasm I proposed it. It is always a guess where your enthusiasm will land you out here. I coaxed a cross old tinner to make the frame for me. He expostulated the while that the thing was impossible, because it had never been done before in this part of the country. It was rather a weird shape, but I left the girls to trim it and went to the church to help decorate. The bell was to follow upon completion. It failed to follow and after waiting an hour or so I sent for it. The girls came carrying one trimmed bell and one half covered. I asked, "Why are you making two wedding-bells?" My answer was, "Why Sensei! must not the groom have one for his head too?"

Everybody wanted to do something for the little maid, for she had so bravely struggled with adversity of fortune and perversity of family. So there were four flower girls, and the music teacher played *at* the wedding march! In spite of her efforts, Lohengrin seemed suffering as it came from the complaining organ.

Miss First River was a lovely enough picture, in her bridal robes of crêpe, to cause the guests to draw in long breaths of admiration, till the room sounded like the coming of a young cyclone. They were not accustomed to such prominence given a bride, nor to weddings served in Western style.

Oh, yes, the groom was there, a secondary consideration for the first time in the history of Hiroshima, but so in love he did not seem to mind the obscurity.

The ceremony over, the newly-wed seated themselves on a bench facing the guests. An elder of the church arose and with a solemnity befitting a burial, read a sermon on domestic happiness and some forty or fifty congratulatory telegrams. After an hour or so of this and several speeches, cake was passed around, and it was over. At the maid's request I gave her an "American watch with a good engine in it" and my blessing with much love in it, and went back to work. Do not for a minute imagine that because I am not a regularly ordained missionary-sister, that I am not working. The fact is, Mate, the missionaries are still afflicted with the work habit, and so subtle is its cheerful influence, it weaves a spell over all who come near. No matter what your private belief is, you roll up your sleeves and pitch right in when you see them at it, and you put all your heart in it and thank the Lord for the opportunity to help.

The fun begins at 5:30 in the morning, to the merry clang of a brazen bell, and it keeps right on till 6 P. M. For fear of getting rusty before sunrise, some of the teachers have classes at night. I would rather have rest. I am too tired, then, to think.

I have put away all my vanity clothes. No need for them in Hiroshima and in an icy room on a winter's morning, I do not stop to think whether my dress has an in-curve or an out-sweep. I fall into the first thing I find and finish buttoning it when the family fire in the dining-room is reached. A solitary warming-spot to a big house is one of the luxuries of missionary life.

In between times I've been cheering up the home sickest young Swede that ever got loose from his native heath. So firmly did he believe that Japan was a land where necessity for work doth not corrupt nor the thief of pleasure break through and steal, he gave up a good position at home and signed a three-years' contract with an oil firm. Now he is so sorry, all the pink has gone out of his cheeks. Until he grows used to the thought that living where the Sun flag floats is not a continuous holiday, the teachers here at school take turns in making life livable for him.

His entertainment means tramps of miles into the country, sails on the lovely Ujina Bay and climbs over the mountains. In the afternoon the boy is so in evidence, we almost fall over him if we step. Yesterday in desperation I tied an apron on him and let him help me make a cake. Even at that, with a dab of chocolate on his cheek and flour on his nose, his summer sky eyes were weepy whenever he spoke of his "Mutter." I have done everything for him except lend him my shoulder to weep on. It may come to that. There is hope, however. One of our teachers is young and pretty.

Jack, in a much delayed epistle, tells me thrilling and awful things about the plague; says he walks through what was once a prosperous village, and now there is not a live dog to wag a friendly tail. Every house and hovel tenantless. Often unfinished meals on the table and beds just as the occupants left them. A great pit near by full of ashes and bones tells the story of the plague come to town, leaving silent, empty houses, and the dust-laden winds as the only mourners.

The native doctors gave a splendid banquet the other night. With the visiting doctors in full array of evening dress and decorations. Jack says it looked like a big international flag draped around the table. Everybody made a speech and Jack has not stopped yet shooting off fireworks in honor of that Englishwoman.

Well, maybe *I* should have studied science. It is too late now. Besides, I have Uncle on my hands, and I have to commit to memory pages on color printing that run like this: "Fine as a single hair or swelling imperceptibly till it becomes a broken play of light and shade or a mass of solid black, it still flows, unworried and without hesitation on its appointed course."

Sada San is coming down next week. I am looking forward to it with great delight and hunting for a plan whereby I can help her.

Suppose Uncle should give me a glad surprise and come too!

Hiroshima.

My dear Best Girl:

If ever a sailor needed a compass, I need the level head that tops your loving heart. I am worried hollow-eyed and as useless as a brass turtle.

It has been days since I heard from Jack. When he last wrote, he was going to some remote district out from

THE LADY AND SADA SAN

Mukden. I dare not think what might happen to him. Says he must travel to the very source of the trouble.

If Jack really wanted trouble he could find it nearer home. Isn't it like him, though, with his German education, to hunt a thing to its lair? I suppose when next I hear from him, he will have disappeared into some marmot hole at the foot of a tree in a Siberian forest.

Sada is here. A pale shadow of her former radiant self. She is in deadly fear of what Uncle has written he expects of her when she returns.

For the first few days of her visit, she was like an escaped prisoner. She played and sang with the girls. The joy of her laughter was contagious. Everybody fell a victim to her gaiety. We have been on picnics up the river in a sampan where we waded and fished, then landed on an island of bamboo and fern and cooked our dinner over a hibachi. We have had concerts, tableaux and charades, here at the school, with a big table for the stage and a silver moon and a green mosquito-net for the scenery.

In every pastime or pleasure, Sada San has been the moving spirit. Adorably girlish and winning in her innocent joy, I grow faint to think of the rude awakening.

She has talked much of Miss West and their life together; their work and simple pleasures.

To the older woman she poured out unmeasured affection, fresh and sweet. Susan made a flower garden of the girl's heart, where, if even a tiny weed sprouted it was coaxed into a blossom. But she gave no warning of the savage storms that might come and lay the garden waste.

Well, I'm holding a prayer-meeting a minute that the rosy ideals of the visionary teacher will hold fast when the wind begins to blow.

I found Sada one day on the bed, a crumpled heap of woe; white and shaking with tearless sobs. Anxious to shield her from the persistent friendliness of the girls, I persuaded her to come with me to the old Prince's garden, just back of the school.

She had heard from Uncle. For the first time he definitely stated his plans. Hara, the rich man, had sent to him a proposal of marriage for Sada! Of course, said Uncle, such an offer from so prosperous and prominent a man must be accepted without hesitation. It was wonderful luck for any girl, said dear Mura, especially one of her birth. Nothing further would be done until she returned, and he wished that to be at once.

Not a suggestion of feeling or sentiment; not a word as to Sada's wishes or rights. If these were mentioned to him, he would undoubtedly reply that the rights in the matter were all his. As to feelings, a young girl had no business with such things. His voice would be courteous, his manner of saying it would fairly puncture the air.

His letter was simply a cold business statement for the sale of the girl. When I looked at the misery in her young eyes, I could joyfully have throttled him and stamped upon him. I wished for a dentist's grinding machine and the chance to bore a nice big hole into each one of his white, even teeth.

She knows nothing of the man Hara except that he is coarse and drinks heavily. The girls in the tea-house always seemed afraid when he came. Vague whispers of his awful life had come to her. What was she to do? She had no money, no place to go, and Uncle was the only relative she had in the world.

Mate, I heard a missionary speak a profound truth, when he said that no Japanese would ever be worth while till all his relatives were dead. Their power is a chain forged around individual freedom.

She had such loving thoughts of Uncle, Sada sobbed, before she came. She longed to make his home happy and be one of his people. She loved the beautiful country of her mother and craved its friendship.

Miss West had drilled it into her conscience that marriage was holy, and impossible without love. (Bless you, Susan!) She wanted to do her duty, but she *could not* marry this man whom she had never seen but once, and had never spoken to.

She knew the absolute power the law of the land gave Uncle over her. She knew the uselessness of a Japanese girl struggling against the rigid rules laid down by her elders. She knew resistance might bring punishment. Well, Mate, I do not care ever to see again such a look as was in Sada's eyes as she turned her set face to me and forced through her stiff lips a stony, "I won't!" But I thanked God for all the Susan Wests and their teachings.

In spite of the girl's unhappiness, there was a thrill in the region of my heart. Of her own free will Sada San had decided. Now there was something definite to work upon. In the back of my brain a plan was beginning to form. Hope glimmered like a Jack-o'-lantern.

It was late evening. A flaming sunset flushed the sky and bathed the ancient garden of arched bridges and twisted trees in a pinkish haze. The very shadows spelled romance and poetry. It was wise to use the charm of the hour for the beginning of my plan.

I drew Sada down beside me, as we sat in a queer little play-house by the garden lake.

In olden times it had been the rest place of the Prince Asano, when he was specially moved to write poetry to the moon as it floated up, a silver ball in a navy-blue sky over "Three Umbrella Mountain." Had his ghost been strolling along then, it would have found deeper things than, "in the sadness of the moon night beholds the fading blossom of the heart," to fill his thoughts.

I led the girl to tell me much of her life in Nebraska; of her friends and their amusements. Hers had been the usual story of any fresh wholesome girl. The social life in a small town had limited her experiences, but had kept her deliciously naïve and sweet.

For the first time in our talks, she avoided Billy's name. I hailed it as a beautiful sign. I mentioned William myself and delighted in her red-cheeked confusion. I gently asked her to tell me of him.

THE LADY AND SADA SAN

She and Billy had gone to school together, played together and he always seemed like a big brother to her. Once a boy had called her a half-breed and Billy promptly knocked him down and sat on his head while he manipulated a shingle.

Another time when they were quite small, the desire of her heart was to ride on the tricycle of a rich little boy who lived across the street. But the pampered youth jeered at her pleadings and exultingly rode up and down before her. Billy saw and bided his time till the small Crœsus was alone. He nabbed him, chucked him in a chicken-coop and stood guard for an hour while Sada rode gloriously.

Through college they were comrades and rivals. Billy had to work his way, for he was the poor son of an invalid mother. From college he had gone straight to a firm of rich manufacturers and was now one of the big buyers.

He had pleaded with her not to come to Japan. He loved her. He wanted her. When she had persisted, he was furious and they had quarreled. But she had thought she was right, then; she did not know how dear Billy was, how big and splendid. She had written to him but seldom, nothing of her disappointment. Maybe he had married. She could not write now. It would be too much like begging, when she was at bay, for the love she had refused when all was well. No, she *could not* tell him.

We talked long and earnestly in that old garden, and the wind that sifted through the pine-needles and the waxy leaves was as gentle as if the spirit of Susan West had come to watch and to bless.

I gained a half promise from her that she would write to Billy at once, but I didn't stop there.

Unsuspected by Sada I learned his full address, and Mate, I wrote a letter to the auburn-haired lover in Nebraska, in which I painted a picture that is going to cause something to happen, else I am mistaken in my estimate of the spirit of the West in general and William Weston Milton in particular.

I told him if he loved the girl to come as fast as steam would bring him; that I would help him at the risk of anything, though I have no idea how. I have just returned from a solitary promenade to the post-office through the dark and lonely streets, so that letter will catch to-morrow's American mail.

Sada told me that for some reason she had never mentioned Billy's name to Uncle. Now isn't that a full hand nestling up my half-sleeve? Uncle thinks the way clear as an empty race-track, and all he has to do is to saunter down the home stretch and gather in the prize-money.

Any scruple on the girl's part will be relentlessly and carelessly brushed aside as a bothersome insect. If she persists, there is always force. He fears nothing from me. I am a foreigner—from his standpoint too crudely frank to be clever.

He doubtless argues, if he gives it any thought, that if I could I would not dare interfere. And then I am so absorbed in color-prints! So I am, and, I pray Heaven, in some way

THE LADY AND SADA SAN

to his undoing. The child has no other friend. Shrinkingly she told me of her one attempt to make friends with some high-class people, and the uncompromising rebuff she had received upon their discovering she was an Eurasian. The pure aristocrats seldom lower the social bars to those of mixed blood. I wonder, Mate, if the ghost of failure, who was her father, could see the inheritance of inevitable suffering he has left his child, what his message would be to those who would recklessly dare a like marriage?

Sada goes to Kioto in the morning. She promises not to show resistance, but to keep quiet and alert, writing me at every opportunity.

I am sure Uncle's delight in securing so rich a prize as Hara will burst forth in a big wedding-feast and many rich clothes for the trousseau. I hope so. Preparation will take time. I would rather gain time than treasure.

I put Sada to bed. Tucked her in and cuddled her to sleep as if she had been my own daughter.

There she lies now. Her face startlingly white against the mass of black hair. The only sign of her troubled day is a frequent half-sob and the sadness of her mouth, which is constantly reading the riot act to her laughing eyes in the waking hours.

Poor girl! She is only one of many whose hopes wither like rose-leaves in a hot sun when met by authority in the form of tyrannical relatives.

The arched sky over the mountain of "Two Leaves" is all a-shimmer with the coming day. Thatched roof and bamboo grove are daintily etched against the amber dawn. Lights begin to twinkle and thrifty tradesmen cheerfully call their wares.

It is a land of peace, a country and people of wondrous charm, but incomprehensible is the spirit of some of the laws that rule its daughters.

Mate dear:

One of my girls, when attached with the blues, invariably says in her written apology for a poor lesson, "Please excuse my frivolous with your imagination, for my heart is warmly." So say I.

I am sending you the crêpes and the kimono you asked for. Write for something else. I want an excuse to spend another afternoon in the two-by-four shop, with a playgarden attached, that should be under a glass case in a jewelry store. The proprietor gives me a tea-party and tells me a few of his troubles every time I go to his store. Formerly he kept two shops exclusively for hair ornaments and ribbons. He did a thriving trade with schoolgirls. Recently an order went out from the mighty maker of school laws to the effect that lassies, high and low, must not indulge in such foolish extravagances as head ornaments. The ribbon market went to smash. The old man could not give his stock away. He stored his goods and went to selling high-priced crêpes, which everybody was permitted to wear. Make another request quickly. I would rather shop than think.

Also, if you need any information as to how to run a cooking-school, I will enclose it with the next package.

Since the war, scores of Japanese women are wild to learn foreign cooking. On inquiry as to the reason of such enthusiasm, we found it was because their husbands, while away from home, had acquired a taste for Occidental dainties. Now their wives want to know all about them so they can set up opposition in their homes to the many tea-houses which offer European food as an extra attraction. And depend upon it, if the women start to learn, they stick to it till there is nothing more to know on the subject.

I was to furnish the knowledge and the ladies the necessary utensils, but I guess I forgot to mention everything we might need.

The first thing we tried was biscuit. All went well until the time came for baking. I asked for a pan. A pan? What kind of a pan? Would a wash pan do? No, if it was all the same I would rather have a flat pan with a rim. Certainly! Here it was with a rim and a handle! A shiny dust-pan greeted my eyes. Well, there was not very much difference in the taste of the biscuit.

The prize accomplishment so far has been pies. Our skill has not only brought us fame, but the city is in the throes of a pie epidemic. A few days ago when the old Prince of the Ken came to visit his Hiroshima home, the cooking-ladies, after a few days' consultation, decided that in no better way could royalty be welcomed than by sending him a lemon pie. They sent two creamy affairs elaborately decorated with meringued Fujis. They were the hit of the season. The old gentleman wrote a poem about them saying he ate one and was keeping the other to take back to his country home when he returned a month hence. Then he sent us all a present.

We have had only one catastrophe. In a moment of reckless adventure my pupils tried a pound cake without a recipe. A pound cake can be nothing else but what it says. That meant a pound of everything and Japanese soda is doubly strong. That was a week ago and we have not been able to stay in the room since.

Good-by! The tailless pink cat and the purple fish with the pale blue eyes are for the kiddies.

I am inclosing an original recipe sent in by Miss Turtle Swamp of Clear Water Village:

Cake.

1 cup of *Desecrated* coconut
5 cup flowers
1 small spoon and barmilla [vanilla]
3 eggs skinned and whipped
1 cup sugar
Stir and pat in pan to cook.

THE LADY AND SADA SAN

Hiroshima, December, 1911.

Mate:

I would be ashamed to tell you how long it is between Jack's letters. He says the activity of the revolutionists in China is seriously interfering with traffic of every kind. All right, let it go at that! Now he has gone way up north of Harbin. In the name of anything *why* cannot he be satisfied? England is with him. I do not know who also is in the party. Neither do I care. I do not like it a little bit. Jealous? The idea. Just plain furious. I am no more afraid of Jack falling in love with another woman than I am of Saturn making Venus a birthday present of one of his rings. The trouble is she may fall in love with him, and it is altogether unnecessary for any other woman to get her feelings disturbed over Jack.

I fail to see the force of his argument that it is not safe nor wise for any woman in that country, and yet for him to show wild enthusiasm over the presence of the Britisher. No, Jack has lost his head over intellect. It may take a good sharp blow for him to realize that intellect, pure and simple, is an icy substitute for love. Like most men he is so deadly sure of one, he is taking a holiday with the other.

Of course you are laughing at me. So would Jack. And both would say it is unworthy. That's just it. It is the measly little unworthies that nag one to desperation. Besides, Mate, I shrink from any more trouble, any more heart-aches as I would from names. The terror of the by-gone years creeps over me and covers the present like a pall.

There is only one thing left to do. Work. Work and dig, till there is not an ounce of strength left for worry. I stay in the kindergarten every available minute. The unstinted friendship of the kiddies over there, is the heart's-ease for so many of life's hurts.

There are always the long walks, when healing and uplift of spirit can be found in the beauty of the country. I tramp away all alone. The little Swede begs often to go. At first I rather enjoyed him. But he is growing far too affectionate. I am not equal to caring for *two* young things; a brokenhearted girl *and* a homesick fat boy are too much for me. He is improving so rapidly I think it better for him to talk love stories and poetry to some one more appreciative. I am not in a very poetical mood. He might just as well talk to the pretty young teacher as to talk about her all the time.

I have scores of friends up and down the many country roads I travel. The boatmen on the silvery river, who always wave their head rags in salute, the women hoeing in the fields with babies on their backs, stop long enough to say good day and good luck. The laughing red-cheeked coolie girls pause in their work of driving piles for the new bridge to have a little talk about the wonders of a foreigner's head. With bated breath they watch while I give them proof that my long hatpins do not go straight through my skull.

The sunny greetings of multitudes of children lift the shadows from the darkest day, and always there is the

THE LADY AND SADA SAN

glorious scenery; the shadowed mystery of the mountains, a turquoise sky, the blossoms and bamboo. The brooding spirit of serenity soon envelops me, and in its irresistible charm is found a tender peace.

On my way home, in the river close to shore, is a crazy little tea-house. It is furnished with three mats and a paper lantern. The pretty hostess, fresh and sweet from her out-of-door life, brings me rice, tea and fresh eel. She serves it with such gracious hospitality it makes my heart warm. While I eat, she tells me stories of the river life. I am learning about the social life of families of fish and their numerous relatives that sport in the "Thing of Substance River"; the habits of the red-headed wild ducks which nest near; of the god and goddesses who rule the river life, the pranks they play, the revenge they take. And, too, I am learning a lesson in patience through the lives of the humble fishermen. In season seven cents a day is the total of their earnings. At other times, two cents is the limit. On this they manage to live and laugh and raise a family. It is all so simple and childlike, so free from pretension, hurry and rush. Sometimes I wonder if it is not we, with our myriad interests, who have strayed from the real things of life.

On my road homeward, too, there is a crudely carved Buddha. He is so altogether hideous, they have put him in a cage of wooden slats. On certain days it is quite possible to try your fortune, by buying a paper prayer from the priest at the temple, chewing it up and throwing it through the cage at the image. If it sticks you will be lucky.

My aim was not straight or luck was against me to-day. My prayers are all on the floor at the feet of the grinning Buddha.

Jack is in Siberia and Uncle has Sada. I have not heard from her since she left. I am growing truly anxious.

January, 1912.

Dearest Mate:

At last I have a letter from Jack. Strange to say I am about as full of enthusiasm over the news he gives me as a thorn-tree is of pond-lilies.

He says he has something like a ton of notes and things on the various stunts of the bubonic germ in Manchuria when it is feeling fit and spry. But he is seized with a conviction that he must go somewhere in northwest China where he thinks there is happy hunting-ground of evidence which will verify his report to the Government. Suppose the next thing I hear he will be chasing around the outer rim of the old world hunting for somebody to verify the Government.

There is absolutely no use of my trying to say the name of the place he has started for. Even when written it looks too wicked to pronounce. It is near the Pass that leads into the Gobi Desert.

Jack wrote me to go to Shanghai and he would join me later. I am writing him that I can't start till the fate of Sada

THE LADY AND SADA SAN

San is settled for better or for worse.

Nankow, China. February, 1912.

Mate:

News of Jack's desperate illness came to me ten days ago and has laid waste my heart as the desert wind blasts life. I have been flying to him as fast as boat and train and cart will take me.

The second wire reached me in Peking last night. Jack has typhus fever and the disease is nearing the crisis. I have read the message over and over, trying to read between the lines some faint glimmer of hope; but I can get no comfort from the noncommittal words except the fact that Jack is still alive. I am on my way to the terminus of the railroad, from where the message was sent. I came this far by train, only to find all regular traffic stopped by order of the Government. The line may be needed for the escape of the Imperial Family from Peking if the Palace is threatened by the revolutionists.

Orders had been given that no foreigner should leave the Legation enclosure. I bribed the room boy to slip me through the side streets and dark alleys to an outside station. I must go the rest of the distance by cart when the road is possible, by camel or donkey when not. Nothing seems possible now. Everything within sight looks as if it had been dead for centuries, and the people walking around have just forgotten to be buried.

I am wild with impatience to be gone but neither bribes nor threats will hurry the coolies who take their time harnessing the donkeys and the camels.

A ring of ossified men, women and children have formed about me, staring with unblinking eyes, till I feel as if I was full of peep holes. It is not life, for neither youth nor love nor sorrow has ever passed this way. The tiniest emotion would shrivel if it dared begin to live. Maybe they are better so. But then, they have never known Jack.

How true it is that one big heart-ache withers up all the little ones and the joy of years as well. With this terror upon me, even Sada's desperate trouble has faded and grown pale as the memory of a dream. Jack is ill and I must get to him, though my body is racked with the rough travel, and the ancient road holds the end of love and life for me.

Around the sad old world I am stretching out my arms to you, Mate, for the courage to face whatever comes, and your love which has never failed me.

Kalgan.

Such wild unbelievable things have happened!

After twenty miles of intolerable shaking on the back of a camel, my battered body fell off at the last stopping-place, which happened to be here. There is no hotel. But three blessed European boys living at this place—agents for a big tobacco firm—took me into their little home. From that time—ten days ago—till now, they have served and cared for me as only sons who have not forgotten their mothers could do.

On that awful night I came, while forcing food on me, they said that Jack had stopped with them on his way out to the desert, where he was to complete his work for the Government. He was to go part of the distance with the English woman, who, with her camels and her guides, was traveling to the Siberian railroad. The next day they heard the whole caravan had returned. Four days out Jack had been taken ill. The only available shelter was an old monastery about a mile from the village. To this he had been moved. My hosts opened a window and pointed to a faraway, high-up light. It was like the flicker of a match in a vast cave of darkness. They told me wonderful things of the rooms in the monastery, which were cut in the solid rock of the mountain-side, and the strange dwarf priest who kept it.

They lied beautifully and cheerfully as to Jack's condition, and all the time in their hearts they knew that he had the barest chance to live through the night.

The woman doctor had nursed him straight through, permitting no one else near. The dwarf priest brought her supplies.

Her last message for the day had been, "The crisis will soon be passed."

Even now something grips my throat when I remember how those dear boys worked to divert me, until my strength revived. They rigged up a battered steamer-chair with furs and bath robes, put me in it, promising that as soon as I was rested they would see what could be done to get me up to the monastery. But I was not to worry. All of them set about seeing I had no time to think. Each took his turn in telling me marvelous tales of the life in that wild country. One boy brought in the new litter of puppies, begging me to carefully choose a name for each. The two ponies were trotted out and put through their pranks before the door in the half light of a dim lantern.

They showed me the treasures of their bachelor life, the family photographs and the various little nothings which link isolated lives to home and love. They even assured me they had had *the* table-cloth and napkins washed for my coming. Household interests exhausted, they began to talk of boyhood days. Their quiet voices soothed me. From exhaustion I slept. When I woke, my watch said one o'clock. The house was heavy with sleeping-stillness.

Through my window, far away the dim light wavered. It seemed to be signaling me. My decision was quick. I would go, and alone. If I called, my hosts would try to dissuade me, and I would not listen. For life or for death, I was going to Jack. The very thought lent me strength and gave my feet cunning stealthiness. A high wall was around the house but, thank Heaven, they had forgotten to lock the gate.

THE LADY AND SADA SAN

Soon I was in the deserted, deep-rutted street shut in on either side by mud hovels, low and crouching together in their pitiful poverty. There was nothing to guide me, save that distant speck of flame. Further on, I heard the rush of water and made out the dim line of an ancient bridge. Half way across I stumbled. From the heap of rags my foot had struck, came moans, and, by the sound of it, awful curses. It was a handless leper. I saw the stumps as they flew at me. Sick with horror, I fled and found an open place.

The light still beckoned. The way was heavy with high, drifted sand. The courage of despair goaded me to the utmost effort. Forced to pause for breath, I found and leaned against a post. It was a telegraph pole. In all the blackness and immeasurable loneliness, it was the solitary sign of an inhabited world. And the only sound was the wind, as it sang through the taut wires in the unspeakable sadness of minor chords. A camel caravan came by, soft-footed, silent and inscrutable. I waited till it passed out to the mysteries of the desert beyond the range of hills.

I began again to climb the path. It was lighter when I crept through a broken wall and found myself in a stone courtyard, with gilded shrines and grinning Buddhas. One image more hideous than the rest, with eyes like glow-worms, untangled its legs and came towards me. I shook with fright. But it was only the dwarf priest—a monstrosity of flesh and blood, who kept the temple. I pointed to the light which seemed to be hanging to the side of the rocks above. He slowly shook his head, then rested it on his hands and closed his eyes. I pushed him aside and painfully crawled up the shallow stone stairs, and found a door at the top. I opened it. Lying on a stone bed was Jack, white and still. A woman leaned over him with her hand on his wrist. Her face was heavily lined with a long life of sorrow. On her head was a crown of snow-white hair. She raised her hand for silence. I fell at her feet a shaking lump of misery.

I could not live through it again, Mate—those remaining hours of agony, when every second seemed the last for Jack. But morning dawned, and with the miracle of a newborn day came the magic gift of life. When Jack opened his eyes and feebly stretched out his hand to me, my singing heart gave thanks to God.

And so the crisis was safely passed. And the hateful science I believed was taking Jack from me, in the skilful hands of a good woman, gave him back to me.

The one comfort left me in the humiliation of my petty, unreasoning jealousy—yes, I *had* been jealous—was to tell her.

And she, whose name was Edith Bowden, opened to me the door of her secret garden, wherein lay the sweet and holy memories of her lover, dead in the long ago.

For forty long and lonesome years she had unfalteringly held before her the vision of her young sweetheart and his work, and through them she had toiled to make real his

THE LADY AND SADA SAN

ideals.

I take it all back, Mate. A career that makes such women as this is a beautiful and awesome thing.

In spite of all my pleadings to come with us, Miss Bowden started once again on her lonely way across the wind-swept plains, back to Europe and her work, leaving me with a never-to-be-forgotten humility of spirit and an homage in my heart that never before have I paid a woman.

I am too polite to say it, but I have had a taste of the place you spell with four letters. Also of Heaven. Just now, with Jack's thin hand safely in mine, I am hovering around the doors of Paradise in the house of the boys in Kalgan. If you could see the dusty little Chinese-Mongolian village, hanging on the upper lip of the mouth of the Gobi Desert, you would think it a strange place to find bliss. But joy can beautify sand and Sodom.

Yesterday my hosts made me take a ride out into the Desert. Oh, Mate, in spots these glittering golden sands are sublime. My heart was so light and the air so rare, it was like flying through sunlit space on a legless horse.

Life, or what answers to it, has been going on in the same way since thousands of years before Pharaoh went on that wild lark to the Red Sea. Every minute I expected to see Abraham and Sarah trailing along with their flocks and their families, hunting a place to stake out a claim, and Noah somewhere on a near-by sand-hill, taking in tickets for the Ark Museum, while the "two by two's" fed below. I never heard of these friends being in this part of the country, but you can never tell what a wandering spirit will do.

Jack is getting fat laughing at me. But Jack never was a lady and does not know what havoc imagination and the spell of the East can play with a loving but lonesome wife. And take it from me, beloved, he never will. Nothing gained in exposing all your follies.

He sends love to you. So do I—from the joyful heart of a woman whose most terrible troubles never happened.

PEKING, February, 1912.

Mate:

I do not know whether I can write you sanely or not. But write you I must. It is my one outlet in these days of anxious waiting. I have just cabled Billy Milton, in Nebraska, to come by the first steamer. I have not an idea what he will do when he gets to Japan, or how I will help him; but he is my one hope.

Yesterday, on our arrival here, I found a desperate letter from Sada San, written hurriedly and sent secretly. She finds that the man Hara, whom her uncle has promised she shall marry, has a wife and three children!

The man, on the flimsiest pretest, has sent the woman home to clear his establishment for the new wife. And, Mate, can you believe it, he has kept the children—the youngest a nursing baby, just three months old!

THE LADY AND SADA SAN

One of the geisha girls in the tea-house slipped in one night and told Sada. She went at once to Uncle and asked him if it was true. He said that it was, and that Sada should consider herself very lucky to be wanted by such a man. Upon Sada telling him she would die before she would marry the man, he laughed at her. Since then she has not been permitted to leave her room.

The lucky day for marriage has been found and set. Thank goodness, it is seventeen days from now, and if Billy races across by Vancouver he can make it. In the meantime Nebraska seems a million miles away. I know the heartbeats of the fellow who is riding to the place of execution, with a reprieve. But seventeen days is a deadly slow nag.

I had already told Jack of my anxiety for Sada San and of the fate that was hanging over her, but now that the blow has suddenly fallen I dare not tell him. In a situation like this I know what Jack would want to do; and in his present weakened condition it might be fatal.

It is useless for me to appeal to anybody out here. Those in Japan who would help are powerless. Those who could help would smile serenely and tell me it was the law. And law and custom supersede any lesser question of right or wrong. By it the smallest act of every inhabitant is regulated, from the quantity of air he breathes to the proper official place for him to die. But, imagine the *majesty* of any law which makes it a ghastly immorality to mildly sass your mother-in-law, and a right, lawful and moral act for a man, with any trumped-up excuse, to throw his legal wife out of the house, that room may be made for another woman who has appealed to his fancy.

Japan may not need missionaries, but, by all the Mikados that ever were or will be, her divorce laws need a few revisions more than the nation needs battleships. You might run a country without gunboats, but never without women.

This case of Hara is neither extreme nor unusual. I have been face to face in this flowery kingdom with tragedies of this kind when a woman was the blameless victim of a man's caprice, and he was upheld by a law that would shame any country the sun shines on. By a single stroke of a pen through her name, on the records at the courthouse, the woman is divorced—sometimes before she knows it. Then she goes away to hide her disgrace and her broken heart—not broken because of her love for the man who has cast her off, but because, from the time she is invited to go home on a visit and her clothes are sent after her, on through life, she is marked. If she has children, the chances are that the husband retains possession of them, and she is seldom, if ever, permitted to see them.

I know your words of caution would be, Mate, not to be rash in my condemnations, to remember the defects of my own land. I am neither forgetful nor rash. I do not expect to reform the country, neither am I arguing. I am simply telling you facts.

I know, too, that some Fountain Head of knowledge will rise from the back seat and beg to state that the new civil code contains many revisions and regulates divorce. The only trouble with the new civil code is that it keeps on containing the revisions and only in theory do they get beyond the books in which they are written.

Next to my own, in my affections, stands this sunlit, flower-covered land which has given the world men and women unselfishly brave and noble. But there are a few deformities in the country's law system that need the knife of a skilled surgeon, amputating right up to the last joint; among these the divorce laws made in ancient times by the gone-to-dust but still sacred and revered ancestors. Who would give a hang for any old ancestor so cut on the bias?

I cannot write any more. I am too agitated to be entertaining.

I wrote Sada a revised version of Blue Beard that would turn that venerable gentleman gray, could he read it. Uncle will be sure to. I dare him to solve the puzzle of my fancy writing. But I made Sada San know the Prince Red Head was coming to her rescue, if the engine did not break down.

Now there is nothing to do but wait and pray there are no weak spots in Billy's backbone.

Cable just received. William is on the wing!

PEKING, CHINA, February, 1912.

Well, here we still are, my convalescent Jack and I, bottled up in the middle of a revolution, and poor, helpless little Sada San calling to me across the waters. Verily, these are strenuous days for this perplexed woman.

It is a tremendous sight to look out upon the incomprehensible saffron-hued masses that crowd the streets. I no longer wonder at the color of the Yellow Sea.

But, Oh, Mate, if I could only make you see the gilded walled city, in which history of the ages is being laid in dust and ashes, while the power that made it is hastening down the back alley to a mountain nunnery for safety! Peking is like a beautiful golden witch clothed in priceless garments of dusty yellow, girded with ropes of pearls. Her eyes are of jade, and so fine is the powdered sand she sifts from her tapering fingers it turns the air to an amber haze; so potent its magic spell, it fascinates and enthralls, while it repels.

For all the centuries the witch has held the silken threads, which bound her millions of subjects, she has been deaf— deaf to the cries of starvation, injustice and cruelty; heedless to devastation of life by her servants; smiling at piles of headless men; gloating over torture when it filled her treasure-house.

Ever cruel and heartless, now she is all a-tremble and sick with fear of the increasing power of the mighty young giant—Revolution. She sees from afar her numbered days. She is crying for the mercy she never showed, begging for time she never granted. She is a tottering despot, a dying tyrant, but still a beautiful golden witch.

We have not been here long but my soul has been sickened by the sights of the pitiless consequences of even the rumors of war all over the country and particularly in Peking. If only the responsible ones could suffer. But it is the poor, the innocent and the old who pay the price for the greed of the others. In this, how akin the East is to the West! The night we came there was a run on the banks caused by the report that Peking was to be looted and burned. Crowds of men, women and even children, hollow-eyed and haggard, jammed the streets before the doors of the banks, pleading for their little all. Some of them had as much as two dollars stored away! But it was the twenty dimes that deferred slow starvation. Banks kept open through the night. Officials and clerks worked to exhaustion, satisfying demands, hoping to placate the mob and avert the unthinkable results of a riot. Countless soldiers swarmed the streets with fixed bayonets. But the bloodless witch has no claim to one single heart-beat of loyalty from the unpaid wretches who wear the Imperial uniform; and when by simply tying a white handkerchief on their arms they go over in groups of hundreds to the Revolutionists, they are only repaying treachery in its own foul coin.

Though I hate to leave Jack even for an hour, I have to get out each day for some fresh air. To-day it seemed to me, as I walked among the crowds, fantastic in the flickering flames of bonfires and incandescent light, that life had done its cruel worst to these people—had written her bitterest tokens of suffering and woe in the deeply furrowed faces and sullenly hopeless eyes.

Earlier in the year thousands of farmers and small tradesmen had come in from the country to escape floods, famine and robber-bands. Hundreds had sold their children for a dollar or so and for days lived on barks and leaves, as they staggered toward Peking for relief.

Now thousands more are rushing from the city to the hills or to the desert, fleeing from riot and war, the strong carrying the sick, the young the old—each with a little bundle of household goods, all camping near the towering gates in the great city wall, ready to dash through when the keeper flings them open in the early morning.

And through it all the merciless execution of any suspect or undesirable goes merrily on. Close by my carriage a cart passed. In it were four wretched creatures with hands and feet bound and pigtails tied together. They were on their way to a plot of crimson ground where hundreds part with their heads. By the side of the cart ran a ten-year-old boy, his uplifted face distorted with agony of grief. One of the prisoners was his father.

I watched the terrified masses till a man and woman of the respectable farmer class came by, with not enough rags on to hide their half-starved bodies. Between them they carried on their shoulders a bamboo pole, from which was swung a square of matting. On this, in rags, but clean, lay a mere skeleton of a baby with beseeching eyes turned to its mother; and from its lips came piteous little whines like a hunger-tortured kitten. Tears streamed down the woman's cheeks as she crooned and babbled to the child in a language only a tender mother knows, but in her eyes was the look of a soul crucified with helpless suffering.

I slipped all the money I had into the straw cradle and fled to our room. Jack was asleep. I got into my bed and covered up my head to shut out the horrors of the multitude that are hurting my own heart like an eternal toothache.

But, honey, bury me deep when there isn't a smile lurking around the darkest corner. Neither war nor famine can wholly eliminate the comical. Yesterday afternoon some audacious youngsters asked me to chaperon a tea-party up the river. We went in a gaily decorated house-boat, made tea on a Chinese stove of impossible shape, and ate cakes and sandwiches innumerable. Aglow with youth and its joys, reckless of danger, courting adventure, the promoters of the enterprise failed to remember that we were outside the city walls, that the gates were closed at sunset and nothing but a written order from an official could open them. We had no such order. When it was quite dark, we faced entrances doubly locked and barred. The guardian inside might have been dead for all he heeded our importunities and bribes. At night outside the huge pile of brick and stone, inclosing and guarding the city from lawless bandits, life is not worth a whistle. A dismayed little giggle went round the crowd of late tea revelers as we looked up the twenty-five feet of smooth wall topped by heavy battlements. Just when we had about decided that our only chance was to stand on each other's shoulders and try to hack out footholds with a bread knife, some one suggested that we try the effect of college yells on the gentlemen within. Imagine the absurdity of a dozen terrified Americans standing there in the heart of China yelling in unison for Old Eli, and Nassau, and the Harvard Blue!

The effect was magical. Curiosity is one of the strongest of Oriental traits, and before long the gates creaked on their hinges and a crowd of slant-eyed, pig-tailed heads peered wonderingly out. The rest was easy, and I heard a great sigh of relief as I marshaled my little group into safety.

Jack's many friends here in Peking are determined that I shall have as good a time as possible. Worried by disorganized business, harassed with care, they always find opportunity not only to plan for my pleasure but see that I have it, properly attended—for of course Jack is not yet able to leave his room.

Beyond the power of any man is the prophecy of what may happen to official-ridden Peking. The air is surcharged with mutterings. The brutally oppressed people may turn at last, rise, and, in their fury, rend to bits all flesh their skeleton fingers grasp.

The Legations grouped around the hotel are triply guarded. The shift, shift, shift of soldiers' feet as they march the streets rubs my nerves like sandpaper.

Rest and sleep are impossible. We seem constantly on the edge of a precipice, over which, were we to go, the fate awaiting us would reduce the tortures of Hades to

THE LADY AND SADA SAN

pin-pricks. The Revolutionists have the railroads, the bandits the rivers. Yet, if I don't reach Japan in twelve days now, I will be too late. Poor Sada San!

Please say to your small son David that his request to send him an Emperor's crown to wear when he plays king, is not difficult to grant. At the present writing crowns in the Orient are not fashionable. As I look out of my window, the salmon-pink walls of the Forbidden City rise in the dusty distance. Under the flaming yellow roof of the Palace is a frail and frightened little six-year-old boy—the ruler of millions—who, if he knew and could, would gladly exchange his priceless crown for freedom and a bag of marbles.

Good night.

PEKING, Next day.

It is Sunday afternoon and pouring rain. Outside it is so drearily mournful, I keep my back turned. At least, the dripping wet will secure me a quiet hour or so.

My Chinese room-boy reasons that only a sure-enough somebody would have so many callers and attend so many functions—not knowing that it is only because Jack's wife will never lack where he has friends. Hence the boy haunts my door ready to serve and reap his reward. But I am sure it was only kindness that prompted him on this dreary day to set the fire in the grate to blazing and arrange the tea-table, the steaming kettle close by, and turn on all the lights. How cozy it is! How homelike!

Jack grows stronger each day, and crosser, which is a good sign. At last I have told him of Sada San's plight; and he is for starting for Kioto to-morrow to "wipe the floor with Uncle Mura," as he elegantly expresses it. But of course he's still too weak to even think of such a journey.

He makes me join in the gaieties that still go on despite the turmoil and unrest. I must tell you of one dinner which, of the many brilliant functions, was certainly unique.

It was a sumptuous affair given by one of the Legation officials. I wore my glory dress—the color Jack loves best. I went in a carriage guarded on the outside by soldiers. Beside me sat a strapping European with his pockets bulging suspiciously. I was not in the least afraid of the threatening mob which stopped us twice.

I could almost have welcomed an attack, just to get behind my big escort and see him clear the way.

Merciful powers! Hate is a sweet and friendly word for what the masses feel for the foreigners, whom most believe to be in league with the Government.

Happily, nothing more serious happened than breaking all the carriage windows; and, in the surprise that awaited me in the drawing-room of the gorgeously appointed mansion, I quite forgot that.

Who should be almost the first to greet me but Dolly and Mr. Dolly, otherwise the Seeker, married and on their honeymoon! She was radiant. And oh, Mate, if you could only see the change in him! As revolutions seem to be in order, Dolly has worked a prize one on him, I think. He was positively gentle and showed signs of the making of a near gentleman. I was glad to see them, and more than glad to see Dolly's unfeigned happiness. The mournful little prince has gone on his way to lonely, isolated Sikkam to take up his task of endless reincarnation.

Very soon I found another surprise—my friend Mr. Carson of the Rockies. It seemed a little incongruous that the simple, unlettered Irishman should have found his way into the brilliant, many-countried company, where were men who made history and held the fate of nations in their hands and built or crumbled empires, and women to match, regally gowned, keen of wit and wisdom.

But, bless you, he was neither troubled nor out of place. He was the essence of democracy and mixed with the guests with the same innocent simplicity that he would have shown at his village church social.

He greeted me cordially, asked after Jack and spoke enthusiastically of his work.

I smiled when I saw that in the curious shuffling of cards he had been chosen as the dinner escort of a tall and stately Russian beauty. I watched them walk across the waxen floor and heard him say to her, "Sure if I had time I would telegraph for me roller skates to guide ye safely over the slickness of the boards." Her answering laugh, sweet and friendly, was reassuring.

For a while it was a deadly solemn feast. The difficulty

was to find topics of common interest without stumbling upon forbidden subjects. You see, Mate, times are critical; and the only way to keep out of trouble is not to get in by being too wordy. By my side sat a stern-visaged leader of the Revolution. Across the way, a Manchu Prince.

Mr. Carson and the beauty were just opposite. I became absorbed in watching her exquisite tact in guiding the awkward hands of her partner through the silver puzzle on each side of his plate to the right eating utensils at the proper time. I saw her pleased interest in all his talk, whether it was crops, cider or pigtails. And for her gentle courtesy and kindness to my old friend I blessed her and wiped out a big score I had against her country. How glad Russia will be!

But the Irishman was not happy. Course after course had been served. With every rich course came a rare wine. Colorado shook a shaggy gray head at every bottle, though he was choking with thirst. He was a teetotaler. Whenever boy No. 1, who served the wine, approached, he whispered, "Water." It got to be "Water, please, *water!*" Then threateningly, "Water, blame ye! Fetch me water." It was vain pleading. At best a Chinaman is no friend to water; and when the word is flung at him with an Emerald accent it fails to arrive. But ten courses without moisture bred desperation; and all at once, down the length of that banquet board, went a hoarsely whispered plea, in the richest imaginable brogue,

"Hostess, *where's* the pump?"

THE LADY AND SADA SAN

It was like a sky-rocket scattering showers of sparks on a lowering cloud. In a twinkling the heaviness of the feast was dispersed by shouts of laughter. Everybody found something delightful to tell that was not dangerous.

We wound up by going to a Chinese theater. When we left, after two hours of death and devastation, the demands of the drama for gore were still so great, assistants had to be called from out the audience to change the scenery and dead men brought to life to go on with the play.

When I got back Jack was, of course, asleep; but he had been busy in my absence. I found a note on my pin-cushion saying he had sent a wire to meet Billy's steamer on its arrival at Yokohama and that I'm to start alone for Japan in a day or two—as soon as it seems safe to travel.

Next day.

Honey, there is a thrill a minute. I may not live to see the finish, for the soldiers have mutinied and joined the mob, maddened with lust for blood and loot. I must tell you about it while I can; for it is not every day one has the chance of seeing a fresh and daring young Republic sally up to an all-powerful dynasty, centuries old with tyranny and treasure, and say, "Now, you vamoose the Golden Throne. It matters not where you go, but hustle; and I don't want any back talk while you are doing it."

If I wasn't so excited I might be nervous. But, Mate, when

you see a cruelly oppressed people winning their freedom with almost nothing to back them but plain grit, you want to sing, dance, pray and shout all at the same time, and there is no mistake about young China having a mortgage on all the surplus nerve of the country. Of course, the mob, awful as it is, is simply an unavoidable attachment of war.

All day there has been terrible fighting, and I am told the streets are blocked with headless bodies and plunder that could not be carried off.

The way the mob and the soldier-bandits got into the city is a story that makes any tale of the Arabian Nights fade away into dull myth.

Some years ago a Manchu official, high in command, espied a beautiful flower-girl on the street and forthwith attached her as his private property. So great was her fascination, the tables were turned and he became the slave—till he grew tired. He not only scorned her, but he deserted her. Though a Manchu maid, the Revolution played into her tapering fingers the opportunity for the sweetest revenge that ever tempted an almond-eyed beauty. It had been the proud boast of her officer master that he could resist any attacking party and hold the City Royal for the Manchus. Alas! he reckoned without a woman. She knew a man outside the city walls—a leader of an organization—half soldiery, half bandits—who thirsted for the chance to pay off countless scores against officers and private citizens inside. After a vain effort to win back her lover, the flower-girl communicated with the captain of the rebel band, who had only been deterred from entering the city by a high wall twenty feet thick. She told him to be ready to come in on a certain night—the gates would be open. The night came. She slipped from doorway to doorway through the guarded streets till she reached the appointed place. Even the sentries unconsciously lent a hand to her plan, in leaving their posts and seeking a tea-house fire by which to warm their half-frozen bodies. The one-time jewel of the harem, who had seldom lifted her own teacup, tugged at the mighty gates with her small hands till the bars were raised and in rushed the mob. She raced to her home, decked herself in all the splendid jewels he had given her, stuck red roses in her black hair, and stood on a high roof and jeered her lover as he fled for his life through the narrow streets.

The city is bright with the fires started by the rabble. The yellow roofs, the pink walls and the towering marble pagodas catch the reflection of the flames, making a scene of barbaric splendor that would reduce the burning of Rome to a feeble little bonfire.

The pitiful, the awful and the very funny are so intermixed, my face is fatally twisted trying to laugh and cry at the same time. Right across from my window, on the street curbing, a Chinaman is getting a hair-cut. In the midst of all the turmoil, hissing bullets and roaring mobs, he sits with folded hands and closed eyes as calm as a Joss, while a strolling barber manipulates a pair of foreign shears. For him blessed freedom lies not in the change of Monarchy to Republic, but in the shearing close to the scalp the hated badge of bondage—his pigtail.

And, Mate, the first thing the looters do when they enter a house is to snatch down the telephones and take them out to burn; for, as one rakish bandit explained, they were the talking-machines of the foreign devils and, if left, might reveal the names of the looters!

High-born ladies with two-inch feet stumble by, their calcimined faces streaked with tears and fright. Gray-haired old men shiver with terror and try to hide in any small corner. Lost children and deserted ones, frantic with fear, cling to any passer-by, only to be shoved into the street and often trampled underfoot. And through it all, the mob runs and pitilessly mows down with sword and knife as it goes, and plunders and sacks till there is nothing left.

As I stood watching only a part of this horror, I heard a long-haired brother near me say, as he kept well under cover, "Inscrutable Providence!" But (my word!) I don't think it fair to lay it all on Providence.

So far the foreign Legations have been well guarded. But there is no telling how long the overworked soldiers can hold out. When they cannot, the Lord help the least one of us.

Jack's friends are working day and night, guarding their property.

I guess the Seeker found more of the plain unvarnished Truth in the East than he bargained for. He and Dolly

THE LADY AND SADA SAN

have disappeared from Peking.

Nobody undresses these nights and few go to bed. Our bodyguard is the room-boy. I asked him which side he was on, and without a change of feature he answered, "Manchu Chinaman. Allee samee bimeby, Missy, I make you tea." I have a suspicion that he sleeps across our door, for his own or our protection, I am not sure which; but sometimes, when the terrible howls of fighters reach me, as I doze in a chair, I turn on the light and sit by my fire to shake off a few shivers, trying to make believe I'm home in Kentucky, while Jack sleeps the sleep of the convalescent. Then a soft tap comes at my door and a very gentle voice says, "Missy, I make you tea." Shades of Pekoe! I'll drown if this keeps up much longer. He comes in, brews the leaves, then drops on his haunches and looks into the fire. Not by the quiver of an eyelash does he give any sign, no matter how close the shots and shouts. Inscrutable and immovable, he seems a thing utterly apart from the tremendous upheaval of his country. And yet, for all anybody knows, he may be chief plotter of the whole movement. His unmoved serenity is about the most soothing thing in all this Hades. I am not really and truly afraid. Jack is with me, and just over there, above the crimson glare of the burning city, gently but surely float the Stars and Stripes.

Good night, beloved Mate. I will not believe we are dead till it happens. Besides, I simply could not die till Jack and I have saved Sada San.

By the way, I start for Japan tomorrow. The prayers of

the congregation are requested!

Kioto Hotel, Kioto Hiroshima, March, 1912.

Beloved Mate:

Rejoice with me! Sing psalms and give thanks. Something has happened. I do not know just what it is, but little thrills of happiness are playing hop-scotch up and down my back, and my head is lighter than usual.

Be calm and I will tell you about it.

In the first place, I got here this morning, more dead than alive, after days of travel that are now a mere blur of yelling crowds, rattling trains and heaving seas. A wire from Yokohama was waiting. Billy had beat me here by a few hours. At noon, to-day, a big broad-shouldered youth met me, whom I made no mistake in greeting as Mr. Milton. Billy's eyes are beautifully brown. William's chin looks as if it was modeled for the purpose of dealing with tea-house Uncles.

Not far from the station is a black-and-tan temple—ancient and restful. To that we strolled and sat on the edge of the Fountain of Purification, which faces the quiet monastery garden, while we talked things over. That is, Billy did the questioning; I did the talking to the mystic chanting of the priests.

I quickly related all that I knew of what had happened to Sada, and what was about to happen. There was no reason

THE LADY AND SADA SAN

for me to adorn the story with any fringes for it to be effective. Billy's face was grim. He said little; put a few more questions, then left me saying he would join me at dinner in the hotel.

I passed an impatient, tedious afternoon. Went shopping, bought things I can never use, wondering all the time what was going to be the outcome. Got a reassuring cable from Jack in answer to mine, saying all was well with him.

Mr. Milton returned promptly this evening. He ordered dinner, then forgot to eat. He did not refer to the afternoon; and long intimacy with science has taught me when not to ask questions. There was only a fragment of a plan in my mind; I had no further communication from Sada, and knew nothing more than that the wedding was only a day off.

We decided to go to Uncle's house together. I was to get in the house and see Sada if possible, taking, as the excuse for calling, a print on which, in an absent-minded moment, I had squandered thirty yen.

Billy was to stay outside, and, if I could find the faintest reason for so doing, I was to call him in. This was his suggestion.

I found Uncle scintillating with good humor and hospitality. Evidently his plans were going smoothly; but not once did he refer to them. I asked for Sada. Uncle smiled sweetly and said she was not in. Ananias died for less! He was quite capable of locking her up in some very quiet spot. I was externally indifferent and internally dismayed. I showed him my print. At once he was the eager, interested artist and he went into a long history of the picture.

Though I looked at him and knew he was talking, his words conveyed no meaning. I was faint with despair. It was my last chance. I could have wagered Uncle's best picture that Billy was tearing up gravel outside. I had been in the house an hour, and had accomplished nothing. Surely if I stayed long enough something had to happen.

Suddenly out of my hopelessness came a blessed thought. Uncle had once promised to show me a priceless original of Hokusai. I asked if I might see it then. He was so elated that without calling a servant to do it for him he disappeared into a deep cupboard to find his treasure.

For a moment, helpless and desperate, I was swayed with a mad impulse to lock him up in the cupboard; but there was no lock.

It was so deadly still it hurt. Then, coming from the outside, I heard a low whistle with an unmistakable American twist to it, followed by a soft scraping sound. My heart missed two beats. I did not know what was happening; nor was I sure that Sada was within the house; but something told me that my cue was to keep Uncle busy. I obeyed with a heavy accent. When he appeared with his print, I began to talk. I recklessly repeated pages of text-books, whether they fitted or not; I fired technical terms at him till he was dizzy with mental gymnastics.

He smoothed out his precious picture. I fell upon it. I raved over the straight-front mountains and the marceled

THE LADY AND SADA SAN

waves in that foolish old woodcut as I had never gushed over any piece of paper before, and I hope I never will again. Not once did he relinquish his hold of that faded deformity in art, and neither did I.

Surely I surprised myself with the new joys I constantly found in the pigeon-toed ladies and slant-eyed warriors. Uncle needed absorption, concentration and occupation. Mine was the privilege to give him what he required.

No further sound from the garden and the silence drilled holes into my nerves. I was so fearful that the man would see my trembling excitement, I soon made my adieux.

Uncle seemed a little surprised and graciously mentioned that tea was being prepared for me. I never wanted tea less and solitude more. I said I must take the night train for Hiroshima. It was a sudden decision; but to stay would be useless.

I said, "Sayonara," and smiled my sweetest. I had a feeling I would never see dear Uncle Mura on earth again and doubtless our environment will differ in the Beyond.

I went to the gate. It faced two streets. Both were empty. Not a sign of Billy nor the jinrickshas in which we had come. I trod on air as I tramped back to the hotel.

HIROSHIMA, Five Days Later, 1912.

Mate dear:

I am back in my old quarters—safe. Why shouldn't I be!

A detective has been my constant companion since I left Kioto, sitting by my berth all night on the train, and following me to the gates of the School!

I had planned to start back to Peking as soon as Sada and Billy were clear and away. But this detective business has made me very wary—not to say weary—and I've had to postpone my return to Jack to await the Emperor's pleasure and lest I bring more trouble on Sada's head, by following too closely on her heels; for I suspect the blessed elopers are themselves on the way to China.

When I took my walk into the country the afternoon after I got here, I saw the detective out of the back of my head, and a merry chase I led him—up the steepest paths I knew, down the rocky sides, across the ferry, and into the remote village, where I let him rest his body in the stinging cold while I made an unexpected call. For once he earned his salary and his supper.

That night I was in the sitting-room alone. A glass door leads out to an open porch. Conscious of a presence, I looked up to find two penetrating eyes fixed on me. It made me creepy and cold, yet I was amused. I sat long and late, but a quiet shadow near the door told me I was not alone. Even when in bed I could hear soft steps under my window.

I have just come from an interview that was deliciously illuminating.

Sada San has disappeared; and, so goes their acute reasoning, as I was the last person in Uncle's house, before her absence was discovered, the logical conclusion is that I have kidnapped her.

Two hours ago the scared housemaid came to announce that "two Mr. Soldiers with swords wanted to speak to me."

I went at once, to find my guardian angel and the Chief of Police for this district in the waiting-room. We wasted precious minutes making inquiries about one another's health, accentuating every other word with a bow and a loud indrawn breath. We were tuning up for the business in hand.

The chief began by assuring me that I was a teacher of great learning. I had not heard it but bowed. It was poison to his spirit to question so honorable, august, and altogether wise a person, but I was suspected of a grave offense, and I must answer his questions.

Where was my home?

Easy.

How did I live?

Easier.

Who was my grandfather?

Fortunately I remembered.

Was I married?

Muchly.

Where was my master?

Did not have any. My husband was in China.

Was I in Japan by his permission?

I was.

Had I been sent home for disobedience? Please explain.

No explanation. I was just here.

Did I know the penalty for kidnaping?

No, color-prints interested me more.

Had any of my people ever been in the penitentiary?

No, only the Legislature.

At this both men looked puzzled. Then the Chief made a discovery.

"Ah-h," he sighed, "American word for crazysylum!"

Would Madame positively state that she knew nothing of the girl's whereabouts. Madame positively and truthfully so stated. I did not know. I only knew what I thought; but, Mate, you cannot arrest a man for thinking. After a grilling of an hour or so they left me, looking worried and perplexed. They had never heard of Billy, and I saw no use adding to their troubles. Nobody seems to have noticed him at dinner with me; and now that I think of it, he had men strange to the hotel pulling the jinrickshas.

It was dear of Billy not to implicate me. I am ignorant of what really happened, but wherever they are I am sure Sada is in the keeping of an honorable man.

Last night, after I closed this letter, I had a cable. It said:

"Married in heaven,
"BILLY AND SADA."

But the cables must have been crossed, for it was dated Shanghai; or else the operator was so excited over repeating such a message he forgot to put in the period.

THE LADY AND SADA SAN

March 15.

Just received a letter from Billy and Sada. It is a gladsome tale they tell. Young Lochinvar, though pale with envy, would bow to Billy's direct method. I can see you, blessed Mate that you are, smiling delightedly at the grand finale of the true love story I have been writing you these months. Billy says on the night it all happened he tramped up and down, waiting for me to call him, till he wore "gullies in the measly little old cow-path they call a street."

The passing moments only made him more furious. Finally he decided to walk right into the house, unannounced, and find Sada if he had to knock Uncle down and make kindling wood of the bamboo doll-house. But as he came into the side garden he saw in the second story a picture silhouetted on the white paper doors. It was Sada and her face was buried in her hands. That settled Billy. He would save Uncle all the worry of an argument by simply removing the cause. There in the dusk, he whistled the old college call, then swung himself up on a fat stone lantern, and in a few minutes he swung down a suitcase and Sada in American clothes. They caught a train to Kobe, which is only a short distance, and sailed out to the same steamer he had left in Yokohama and which arrived in Kobe that day.

Billy says, for a quick and safe wedding ceremony commend him to an enthusiastic, newly-arrived young missionary; and for rapid handling of red tape connected with a license, pin your faith to a fat and jolly American consul. So that was what the blessed rascal was doing all that afternoon he left me in Kioto to myself. Cannot you see success in life branded on William's freckled brow right now?

The story soon spread over the ship. Passengers and crew packed the music-room to witness the ceremony, and joyously drank the health of the lovers at the supper the Captain hastily ordered. Without hindrance, but half delirious with joy, they headed for Shanghai.

Billy found that he could transact a little business in China for the firm at home and with Western enterprise decided to make his honeymoon pay for itself.

And now that my task is finished I shall follow them as fast as the next steamer can carry me.

PEKING, April, 1912.

Back once again, Mate, in the City of Golden Dusts. Glorious spring sunshine, and the whole world wrapped in a tender haze. Everything has little rainbows around it and the very air is studded with jewels.

Soldiers are still marching; flags are flying; drums are thumping and it is all to the tune of Victory for the Revolutionists. But best of all Jack is well! To me Peking is like that first morning of Eve's in the Garden of Eden.

THE LADY AND SADA SAN

What crowded, happy weeks these last have been. Waiting for Jack; amusing him when time hangs heavy—even unto reading pages of scientific books with words so big the spine of my tongue is threatened with fracture.

And in between times? Well, I am thanking my stars for the chance to doubly make up for any little tenderness I may have passed by. Put it in your daily thought book, honey, forevermore I am going to remember that if at the time we'd use the strength in doing, that we consume afterwards being sorry we didn't do, life would run on an easy trolley.

Billy and Sada are with us, still with the first glow of the enchanted garden over them. Bless their happy hearts! I am going to give them my collection of color prints to start housekeeping with. How I'd *love* to see Uncle—through a telescope.

To-night we are having our last dinner here. To-morrow the four of us turn our faces toward the most beautiful spot this side of Heaven, home. The happy runaways to Nebraska, Jack and I to the little roost we left behind in Kentucky.

There goes the music for dinner. It's something about "dreamy love." Love isn't a dream, Mate—not the kind I know; it's all of life and beyond.

I know what they are playing!

Breathe but one breath

Rose beauty above
And all that was death
Grows life, grows love,
Grows love!

THE END